D0227291

PICNIC IN IRAQ

PHILIP CAINE

PICNIC IN IRAQ

Copyright © 2015: PHILIP CAINE. All rights reserved.

First paperback edition printed 2015 in the United Kingdom

ISBN 978-0-9933748-0-7

No part of this book shall be reproduced or transmitted in any form
or by any means,
electronic or mechanical, including photocopying, recording, or by
any information retrieval
system without written permission of the publisher.

Published by PHILIP CAINE
philcaine777@hotmail.com

For more copies of this book, please email:
philcaine777@hotmail.com

Cover Design: www.gonzodesign.co.uk

Printed in Great Britain by:
Orbital Print www.orbitalprint.co.uk

Although every precaution has been taken in the preparation of this
book, the publisher and
author assume no responsibility for errors or omissions. Neither is
any liability assumed for
damages resulting from the use of this information contained.

ABOUT THE AUTHOR

Philip has over thirty five years' experience, operating projects across three continents, within the Oil & Gas Industry. He worked the pioneering years of the North Sea, for over fifteen years on Oil Rigs, Barges & Platforms, then moved to onshore projects, spending three years in North & West Africa. Seven years were spent operating in the 'Former Soviet Union' where he managed multiple projects in Kazakhstan & Russia..

The end of the Iraq War in 2003 produced a change of client that took Philip to Baghdad, where he directed the operations and project management, of multiple accommodation bases for the American Military in Baghdad and Northern Iraq.

Philip semi-retired in 2014 and began writing in February 2015. PICNIC IN IRAQ is his first novel.

'I learned that courage was not the absence of fear, but the triumph over it.
The brave man is not he who does not feel afraid, but he who conquers that fear.'

Nelson Mandela

We few, we happy few, we band of brothers.
For he to-day that sheds his blood with me, shall be my brother; be he 'er so vile,
for this day shall gentle his condition.
And gentlemen in England now-a-bed, shall think themselves accursed, they were not here.
And hold their manhoods cheap, while any speaks, that fought with us, upon Saint Crispin's day."

William Shakespeare, 'Henry V'

Prologue

The huge steel door swung silently open, revealing a long narrow room, ten metres by fifty. The polished steel floor shimmered in the soft blue glow of the concealed lighting and the air was pleasantly chilled by a silent a/c system.

Cellophane-wrapped bundles of bank notes were neatly stacked onto chrome shelving, which ran the length of both side walls. A long central raised platform held piles of gold and platinum ingots in clear plastic cases. At the end of the vault was a row of polished steel cupboards.

The Iraqi colonel looked into the vault and nodded slowly, a sinister smile on his tanned face, his dark eyes wide in expectation. He turned and slapped the expensively dressed Kuwaiti hard across his face, almost knocking him off his feet. The man held his composure and stood upright; his shoulders back in defiance, as a trickle of blood ran from the corner of his bottom lip. He took the white handkerchief from his breast pocket and dabbed at the wound. The colonel made a sweeping, almost polite gesture with his hand, inviting the man to enter the room, the sinister smile ever present.

The pair slowly walked the length of the room and stopped in front of the steel cupboards. Again the colonel offered the feigned polite hand gesture, directing the Kuwaiti to unlock the doors. The man took a Chubb key from his waistcoat pocket and dutifully moved along the row, unlocking each in turn.

The Kuwaiti stood back, his head upright; his defiant stance resumed and continued dabbing at his lip. The colonel stepped forward and opened the nearest cupboard, as concealed lighting illuminated the interior. Twenty shallow Perspex drawers filled the cupboard from top to bottom. He slid open a drawer to reveal dozens of small white paper packets. Removing one, he carefully opened the tiny bundle. His thick black moustache twitched, as his sinister smile widened into a huge grin.

Chapter One
February 1991
'Colonel Omar'

The Bentley was doing over a hundred and forty kilometres an hour at the head of the convoy. The old general in the back seat, puffed on a large Cuban Monte Cristo and blew grey smoke rings forward, then watched them dissipate around the drivers head. He sipped Hennessey XO from a Baccarat crystal brandy balloon and luxuriated in the comfort of the three hundred thousand dollar vehicle. A large wad of ash fell onto the seat beside him and he swiftly brushed it off with the back of his hand, leaving a dull grey smear on the soft white leather. *I'll have it valeted*, he thought, *before I give it to Saddam.*

Following behind were Rolls Royces, Ferraris, Lamborghinis; all in all about two hundred luxury cars and 4x4's, carrying over six hundred of Saddam Hussein's Republican Guard north along the main highway, from the Kuwaiti border to Baghdad. The vehicles and contents were part of the plunder the Iraqi army had stolen from Kuwait, subsequent to their invasion of this tiny adjacent country. The Kuwaitis had not been any match for Saddam's hordes pouring over the border, which left the richest city in the Middle East exposed and vulnerable. The Iraqi army had raped and pillaged to biblical proportions during their six months occupation. It was not until the US led coalition eventually agreed to intervene and rescue little Kuwait, that the Iraqis had decided fighting the Americans was not an option. The invaders had loaded as much as was possible of Kuwait's moveable wealth onto army trucks, lorries and stolen vehicles and ran for the border and Iraq.

Colonel Omar Khalid al Muttah was in a top of the range Toyota Landcruiser with three other Republican Guards; a major and two captains and theirs was the last vehicle in the convoy. They had left Kuwait as swiftly as they had moved in and the only items in their vehicle, other than weapons, were two large insulated picnic boxes. The convoy stretched for almost four kilometres and was moving fast when the Tomahawk missile exploded and destroyed the first forty vehicles. Colonel Omar saw the explosion in the distance and knew there would be more.

'Get the hell off this road,' he screamed at the driver.

The big vehicle lurched and almost toppled as it went down the banking and onto the hard surface of the compacted sand. The driver, with foot hard down on the accelerator, pushed the powerful engine to maximum revs. The second Tomahawk hit and decimated the middle of the convoy; the third and fourth missiles finished off the rear of the column. Omar looked back and the whole highway was ablaze, nothing was left of the convoy, vehicles or men.

They pushed on at top speed into the desert, slowing down as the air assault appeared to be over. They drove for about twenty minutes in a north easterly direction and came upon a small remote clump of bushes and trees, with a large pond in the middle. The 'oasis' was about the size of a tennis court and the water in the pond was cloudy and somewhat fetid. They parked the vehicle under one of the trees and dismounted. Going to the back of the vehicle they opened a case of water, each taking a litre bottle and after quenching their thirst, poured the remainder over their faces and discarded the empty bottles.

'We need to hide these,' said the colonel, as he tapped the two picnic boxes.

His companions nodded agreement and they looked to the pond in unison. One of the captains waded into the murky water and found it was firm under foot. It was shallow around the edge, but sloped away towards the middle. He made his way to the centre of the pond and the water depth had reached his chest, a good five feet deep. The bottom of the pond was still firm and he shouted to the colonel,

'This will be a safe place to hide them, sir,'

The captain returned to the Landcruiser and the four men lifted the boxes from the vehicle and carried them to the edge of the water.

'Open one.' said the colonel.

One of the captains unclipped the lid and stood back. The colonel bent down and took four small packets from the box and handed one packet to each of the men, putting the fourth in his pocket. 'These will tide us over until we return,' he said with a smile.

The captain closed the box and picked it up. The second captain lifted the other and they both waded out into the centre of the small lake. Letting the heavy boxes sink, they were confident they would be secure here.

They returned to the shade of the trees and Omar removed a map from a pouch on his body armour; took a compass bearing and map reading and marked the location clearly on the map, along with a small notation, smiling as he did so. Omar picked up one of the discarded water bottles, shook out any drops of liquid; rolled up the map and pushed it into the bottle, securing the top firmly.

'Remove the rear door inside panel,' he said to no one in particular.

The second captain took out a multi-tool and did as he had been instructed. The colonel then concealed the map behind the panel and the captain screwed it back into place. The four men looked at each other and smiled.

'We'll wait until dark and then get back to the highway,' announced Omar.

He turned and went to the front passenger seat, deftly removed his AK47 and turned sharply to the three men. Swiftly cocking the weapon, he cut them down with a prolonged burst of fire. He stood for a few seconds, his breathing calm and then checked them all to ensure they were dead. He knelt at each body in turn and retrieved the packets he had given them a few moment before. The colonel did not want to leave the bodies at the oasis. There was no time nor did he have the inclination to dig a mass grave. Returning to the rear of the vehicle, he opened the floor panel and removed the long towrope from the spare wheel compartment. Then, after the unpleasant task of dragging the bodies next to each other, tied each of them in turn, to the towrope. He clipped the other end of the rope to the towing bracket, under the rear of the Landcruiser.

Omar closed up the back of the vehicle, looked at the men again, slowly walked to the driver's seat and climbed in. His exertions had caused him to sweat profusely and his shirt was clinging to his back, soaked with perspiration. His pulse was steady, as he considered what he had done, but the contents of the boxes quickly washed away remorse. He started the engine and drove North West, towards the highway. In the rear view mirror, he watched to make sure his three colleagues were still attached to the rope. Dust and sand rose from the grizzly cargo, as it was dragged behind the vehicle. The arms and heads bounced from side to side, in a dance of death. He drove for about five kilometres and decided he was far enough away from the oasis, to leave the bodies. He stopped the vehicle, went to the rear and unhooked the towrope. He looked at the gruesome remains of his colleagues, their uniforms shredded, their arms and faces stripped of skin and flesh. He turned away and climbed back into the comfort and luxury of the Landcruiser, started the engine and continued the short drive back to the motorway. For a few moments, he considered the men he had left to rot in the desert sand; then his thoughts returned to the two picnic boxes at the bottom of the oasis. Just how much would twenty kilos of diamonds be worth?

* * *

The sun had set and twilight was approaching, he was heading north now and pushing the vehicle hard towards Baghdad. The city was about three hundred kilometres away and the thought of driving through the night did not give him any comfort, but he knew the Americans were behind him. There was no alternative.

He thought of the diamonds and how they would enable him to get his family out of Iraq and away from that crazy bastard, Saddam. His family had been one of the most respected in Iraq, when Hussein had taken power, all those years ago. Now, Omar was no more than a Ba'athist puppet, serving a mad man. He disliked what he had become and wanted to return to a life of honour. The diamonds would be his ticket to South America and a new life for his family.

The vehicle was travelling so fast, the explosion from the small roadside bomb, only caught the offside front wing, the window and the tyre; if it had been any bigger it would have taken the vehicle out altogether. Omar held onto the steering wheel and tried to keep the big vehicle on the road, but at that speed and with no front tyre, he was at the mercy of the laws of physics and the Landcruiser spun into an uncontrollable dance, smashing the colonel against the side window. His head split open and he lost consciousness.

Chapter Two
'CIA'

'How you feeling, sir?' the voice was American. Omar opened his eyes and the glaring light above him, made him wince. When his vision had cleared, he realised he was in a large tent, with several other wounded men. The strong smell of disinfectant was somewhat sickly and the hum from the overhead fluorescent lighting did nothing to help the pain in his head.

'How are you feeling, Colonel?' the American said again. 'What's your name, sir?'

'Where am I?' said Omar.

'You're in an American field hospital.'

'Yes I realise that, but where?'

'You're in Kuwait, sir.'

The medic held a small beaker of water to the colonel's mouth and Omar took a couple of sips.

'You were found three days ago, by one of our forward recon patrols. You were brought here and have been out ever since. You've a very bad concussion, some cuts and bruising, but nothing that won't heal. You're very lucky.'

Omar felt anything but lucky.

'I am Colonel Omar Khalid al Muttah,' he said in perfect English, 'And I do not intend to say anything further.'

The medic helped him to drink a little more water.

'That's okay, sir, I'm just a medic, there'll be other guys who'll be talking to you once you're well enough.'

Omar's heart dropped as he considered his situation, he was now very concerned about what may be in store for him. He vaguely remembered the explosion and then the map in the back door of the Landcruiser

'Oh no,' he said out loud.

The pain in his head increased, as his blood pressure rose. Then welcome relief came, as he slipped into unconsciousness again.

* * *

Omar had been brought to a small interrogation room. He had been given clean underclothes, a new orange coverall and canvas slip-ons. The two marines with him looked very tough and unfriendly, although they had been polite and courteous to him during the transfer from the medical facility to this place.

'Where am I, please?'

No response from the statue like marines. With a little difficulty, due to the manacles round his waist and wrists, he sipped some water from a plastic bottle, as the door opened and two men entered.

'Good afternoon, Colonel Muttah,' said the first man. They sat down on the opposite side of the table and looked at him for several seconds.

'Wait outside, please,' said the other, to the marines.

'Where am I and who are you?' said Omar. 'You are not in uniform, so I assume you are CIA,' he continued.

'Where you are and who we are is not important at this time, but you can call me Mr Brown and this is Mr Green,' the first man gestured to his colleague.

Definitely CIA he thought.

'How are you feeling?' said Brown.

Omar sat back on the metal chair and looked round the room in despair, no windows, dull lighting and an unpleasant smell. The poor air-conditioning was making him sweat, in the uncomfortable orange coverall. His head was causing him great pain and the staples across his scalp, were itching under the tightly wrapped bandage. He had been given codeine for the pain, but it was not working.

'We know your name and rank, colonel,' said Brown, 'We know you are Republican Guard, but we want to know what your orders were, while you occupied Kuwait?'

'We also need to know what you were taking back to Baghdad with you?' added Mr Green.

'I am a prisoner of war and demand to be treated as such,' said Omar.

'You are a suspected war criminal, colonel, I'm afraid military protocols are not going to help you here, sir.'

'Where exactly is here?'

'You're still in Kuwait, but you will be moved to another facility outwith the Middle East, as soon as possible,' said Brown.

Omar was worried now. His head was giving him more pain than he could bear, as he fought to keep his wits about him. He struggled with the water bottle again, gulped a mouthful, refreshing his dry throat. He quickly considered his options; they were few indeed and if they did move him to a foreign country, God knows when, or if, he would get back to Baghdad. His instinct for self-preservation overcame his desire for wealth. He would negotiate a deal for his release and the return of the diamonds would be his ticket home.

'Gentlemen, if I were to help you, are you in a position, do you have the authority, to help me?'

'Anything you tell us will work in your favour, Colonel. But whether it will get you home, depends on just how valuable the information is.'

Omar felt there was a glimmer of hope and although the loss of the diamonds hurt, the loss of his freedom, or worse, was not an option.

'My head is giving me a lot of pain; do you think I could have some more painkillers please?'

'Marine,' shouted Mr Brown.

The door opened swiftly and the two big soldiers rushed in.

'Calm down,' said Green, as he raised his hand to the soldiers.

'Get some painkillers for the colonel please and more water.'

'Sir, yes, sir,' barked the bigger of the two soldiers and they left the room

'So, Colonel, what valuable information might you have?'

'I am not quite sure what the actual value is gentlemen,' smiled Omar, 'But if I could lead you to twenty kilos of diamonds, would that improve my situation?'

Brown and Green looked at each other and Omar could sense their change in mood, as slight smiles appeared on their faces. Brown took a small clear Ziploc bag from his pocket and opened it. The contents tinkled onto the steel table, lighting up the dull room with a thousand sparkles.

'Go on, Colonel, we're listening.'

The colonel nodded and smiled for the first time, 'I see you checked my pockets.'

'Yes indeed, Colonel,' said Brown,' also smiling, 'Please go on.'

'Several months ago I acquired a large amount of diamonds from the Reserve Bank of Kuwait. When the Americans decided to intervene and our withdrawal to

Iraq was imminent, I and three others moved the stones in two picnic boxes.'

There was a knock on the door and the big marine entered. He placed the medication and water in front of Omar, stood to attention, turned smartly and left. The colonel took the tablets and washed them down awkwardly, his manacles rattling as he did so.

'Please go on, sir,' said Green, in a somewhat friendlier tone.

'We managed to escape from a convoy that was destroyed in an airstrike and we hid the
 boxes in the southern desert.'

'What happened to the other three men with you?' said Brown.

'They are dead,' replied Omar, looking at the concrete floor between his feet.

'So where exactly are these picnic boxes?'

'There is a map with the location and grid reference.'

'And where is the map, Colonel?'

Omar leaned forward and struggled to drink the water; as several drops of blood dripped from his nose onto the table in front of him. He groaned as he looked at the two men opposite, his eyes rolled upwards and he slumped back in the chair.

'Are you alright, Colonel?' said Brown.

'Marine! Get a medic in here. Now!'

Omar's body went into spasm and then lurched forward onto the steel table, his shoulders shaking uncontrollably. Brown rushed round the table and was holding his head, as the convulsions suddenly stopped. The door burst open and the medic rushed in. After feeling the carotid artery, he checked the colonel's eyes, then turned to Brown, 'This man is dead, sir.'

Chapter Three
'Gift from God'

Salim Al Kahlil's face looked seventy years old, but in truth he was twenty years younger. He was hard working and intelligent and his weather-beaten skin and deep set black eyes were evidence of living his whole life in the desert. If he had only travelled fifty kilometres to the east or west, he would have found the Euphrates or Tigris Rivers and life would have been easier and gentler for him and his family. He had rarely moved from the tiny village, with its gaggle of families existing in their self-made hovels of mud and rusty corrugated sheeting, a few makeshift shops and a small building that doubled as a school and Mosque.

Salim heard them before he saw them; the dust cloud was coming closer and the sound, like thunder, grew louder. He, being a simple man, was afraid and swiftly gathered his family together in the small shack. The other villagers too felt the same impending danger and began collecting their children and various small animals into their respective homes. The dust cloud began to engulf the cluster of tiny dwellings and the sound now, was almost deafening. As Salim stood at the door, he watched as scores of huge tanks, their enormous barrels pointing skywards rumbled past. Trucks of various sizes loaded with soldiers followed, all heading north.

In the days that followed, Salim spent many hours thinking what must be happening in the south and great concern fell upon him. He no longer felt safe in his home and perhaps this was the time to move his family north to a safer environment, perhaps to Baghdad. He talked with his wife Nabila and she was surprised he could think of such possibilities and even consider leaving the tiny village,

'What will become of us, Salim?'

'We will make a new and better life for us and our sons. Have no fear.'

He was determined and after three days of persuasion and more trucks and vehicles passing the village, Nabila agreed. Salim knelt on the floor and embraced his sons. Their eyes fixed on him in anticipation. Holding them close, he announced,

'We are going to leave this place and go north to the great city of Baghdad.'

The excitement in the bright faces of the boys gave him great joy and strengthened his resolve. He stood up and drew Nabila to him, 'You see, our sons are happy to leave and God will protect us.'

It had not taken them long to pack their belongings and the four bundles wrapped in thin, almost worn out rugs stood in the centre of their tiny house. Salim had no idea how far away Baghdad was, or how long it would take to get there. He was happy and heartened, as he loaded the small rickety wooden cart with their bundles. He harnessed the old donkey and helped Nabila onto the wooden box that served as a seat; he kissed her hand and said with a smile,

'All will be well.'

The sons excitedly piled on top of the bundles and Salim took the bridle of the aged donkey in his calloused hand.

'Allah o Akbah,' he shouted as he pulled the donkey and began their long trek toward the north.

* * *

They walked for five days and had no idea they were still three hundred kilometres south of Baghdad. Salim and the boys made a small encampment in a cluster of trees, about two hundred metres from the road and had settled down to their meagre evening meal, when suddenly they heard an explosion. Salim stood and looked towards the sound and flash, coming from the direction of the road. Nabila instinctively gathered her sons close to her and said,

'What is it, Salim?'

'I don't know, I must go and see what has happened,' he said.

'Salim, it is not our concern.' But after several more minutes of argument she agreed, 'Very well if you must go, please wait until first light.'

The family settled down for the night. Salim slept fitfully, being woken just as dawn was breaking, by the sound of vehicles and voices coming from the direction of the road. He looked and saw several military vehicles, but these were not Iraqi soldiers; they were taking what looked like a man's body from a big white vehicle that had crashed off the highway. A few minutes later he heard another unfamiliar noise and a helicopter came into sight, slowly touching down in a cloud of dust, close to the military vehicles. The body of the man was carried to the helicopter and as swiftly as it appeared, it vanished into the cool morning sky. The soldiers returned to their vehicles and were gone from sight within a few minutes.

Nabila was standing by him now, even more fearful than usual.

'I don't think you should go, Salim, I know I agreed, but it's too dangerous.'

'I promise to be careful,' he said, as he let go her arm and began walking towards the road. At the roadside, he could clearly see the explosion he had heard, was the cause of the crash. The front wing was blackened and buckled, the tyre was shredded and the side windows had gone. He looked inside the vehicle and saw the dried blood on the seat and door, repelled he still climbed in. The keys were in the ignition and, as he turned them, the engine burst into life. He switched off the engine, went to the rear of the vehicle and found the tools and jack under the rear floor. After struggling to remove the heavy spare wheel, he finally managed to roll it round to the front and began the task of replacing the damaged one. Nabila could see him at the side of the big white truck, but was unsure what he was doing. She watched him climb back inside and a few seconds later the truck was moving and coming towards her. When the truck stopped Salim jumped out and with a grand gesture of his arms and huge grin on his face, proudly showed his family what he had found.

'Pack everything into the back and let's go,' he instructed, excitedly.

'How can you take this truck, Salim, it is not ours to take,' said Nabila.

'If the truck was that important the soldiers would not have left it, God has helped us, it is a gift, so we will not refuse it, now let's go.'

As he pulled off the desert and onto the road, he was happy his family had already found such great fortune; it was beyond his dreams. If only he knew, the plastic bottle hidden in the back door, held a map to riches beyond anyone's dreams?

Chapter Four
Spring 2008
'Welcome to Baghdad'

Nasir was twenty four years old, a student of medicine and the eldest son of four. He had come to Baghdad many years before with his family. His father had placed him in a good school. He had worked hard and became a diligent, caring young man. Eventually he had been accepted into Baghdad's Medical University and had made great progress. His family were proud of him. But in the back rooms of the mosque, after Friday prayers, he had been taught by radical thinkers and his mind had been corrupted. He no longer believed in the true Muslin faith, a faith of belief and charity and love. He had been indoctrinated with hate, resentment and anger.

As he sat in the driver's seat of the old Nissan, he did not feel the cold chill of the morning air. The souk was filling up, as crowds of customers pushed around the street vendors. Children laughed as they walked to school, car horns sounded and another day had begun in the vibrant Baghdad market place. Nasir looked around him, his eyes registering nothing and everything. He looked to the clear blue sky through the filthy cracked windscreen and felt at peace with himself, almost serene.

The small American convoy was moving slowly towards him, through the tightly packed pedestrians. As the second of the three vehicles was alongside the Nissan, Nasir smiled, closed his eyes and gently whispered,

'Allah O Akbah,' as he depressed the switch in his hand. The feel of the switch under his thumb was the last thing he ever felt.

The sound of the explosion reverberated across the shimmering water of the Tigris and through the Green Zone. First, the sirens of ambulances and fire tenders, then the sound of the Blackhawks overhead, indicated air-cover had arrived above the carnage in the busy market place. The scene was total devastation, shop windows shattered, stalls destroyed and the foul smell of burned and scorched flesh hung in the air. The bomb had gone off just after seven a.m. with hundreds of people in the market, resulting in maximum impact. Sitting at the bottom of a small blast crater the old Nissan was nothing more than a blackened tangled mess, about 20% of its original size. Blooded people and bodies were everywhere, screams from the wounded, moans from the dying, silence from the dead.

* * *

In his Green Zone accommodation, Jack Castle rose quickly from his bed and listened for more explosions. His mind alert and tuned to the noises of this desperate city, a skill he had learned over the last five years, while providing private security in this tortured town. He opened his cabin door and sucked in the cool morning air. He listened for more explosions, but only the murmur of the camp generators and the sound of birds in the trees broke the silence. He closed the door, picked up a towel and went into the bathroom.

In his early fifties, he was tall, reasonably fit and healthy; although shedding several pounds would not go amiss. Greying hair complemented sparkling brown eyes that gave a light to his tanned face. He had a good sense of humour and an infectious personality that most people liked. His happy childhood had been spent in England's Lake District and he was the elder of two brothers. His father and mother had been doctors in Windermere. It was his father who had taught Jack the meaning and value of responsibility, friendship, loyalty and honour. Love, kindness and respect, were the gifts his mother had endowed him with. He was occasionally short tempered and quick to anger, but equally as quick to forgive.

* * *

On his twentieth birthday, his life had changed dramatically. He had returned home from Edinburgh, where he attended medical college. His father had picked him up from the rail station and drove him home, to the big Tudor style house on the edge of Lake Windermere. His mother was in the garden with the dogs, as the Jaguar entered the gates and slowly drove up to the house. As Jack stepped from the car, his mother hugged and smothered him with birthday kisses. The two Labradors scurried around his feet, almost tripping him up. Mathew, his younger sibling by a couple of years, came out and the two brothers embraced and then shook hands. They were the best of friends and would soon be students together, when Mathew started the same medical school, later in the year. The early spring day was cool, but with clear sky and bright sunshine; a rare event indeed for the English Lake District. The plan for the day was lunch with the family and in the evening, the boys would be out for a few beers with their friends.

Lunch had been enjoyed on the balcony of the Windermere Lodge Hotel, overlooking the lake. His father had let him drive the Jaguar back to the house, always a great joy for Jack to get behind the wheel of the beautiful car. He was not driving excessively quickly, in fact he was positively slow, as he wound his way along the narrow road, which ran the length of the lake. The delivery truck was moving far too fast for the winding country lane. As it turned the tight bend, it hit the Jaguar on the front offside, with enough force to send the big car through the small drystone wall, at the side of the road.

The momentum took it down the steep embankment. As the car spun sideways, it slammed into a big oak, then bounced off and careered down the slope, smashing into a large rock formation at the water's edge. The vehicle rolled into the lake and began to sink slowly. Jack was fully conscious all the way down. The car had come to rest upside down, in about eight feet of water. He had struggled to open his door and then managed to slip out and over the underside of the vehicle, burning his hands, as he pulled himself over the hot steaming exhaust pipe. His father was unconscious, but he saw Mathew and his mother were moving. His breath was almost gone as he pulled open the smashed door and dragged his father out of the front seat and up to the surface. He saw Mathew surface and fully expected him to return and save their mother.

Jack had pulled his father to the bank, but quickly realised he was dead. He saw his brother drag himself up the bank and realising Mathew was not going back for their mother; dove back into the lake and down to the upturned car. His mother was pounding on the window, her eyes wide, as she struggled for breath. He pulled on the buckled door for several seconds, but it was jammed tight. His breath was almost gone, so he pushed upwards, gulping air, as he broke the surface. Then diving down again, this time to the other side of the car and through the window his brother had exited a few moments earlier. His mother was unconscious now, but he managed to drag her petite body through the open window, out of the stricken Jaguar and up to the surface. Mathew had recovered his senses and was in the water, pulling their mother to the bank. People were running down the embankment to help, but it was too little too late. Jack gave his mother mouth to mouth for several minutes, until the dreadful realisation hit him; she too was dead. He went to his father and checked him again, his neck had been broken. At least he had died swiftly, unlike his mother.

In the two weeks prior to the funeral, Jack became resentful, angry and withdrawn. His feelings of guilt grew, as he blamed himself for the loss of his parents. He blamed his brother for not rescuing their mother. He hated his weakness at not being able to save her. The day after the funeral, he had left the beautiful home on the edge of the lake and joined the British army. It was there, he had found a way to deal with the demons that plagued his existence. He worked hard and swiftly rose through the ranks, to the level of captain in the Special Air Service.

After fifteen years in the military, he was offered an opportunity to move into the lucrative world of private security.

* * *

Jack showered and dressed. Checked his laptop for overnight emails and messages, responded to the urgent ones, saved the less important and deleted the insignificant. He took the body armour from the wall rack and deftly slipped it over his head, fastened down the sides and secured the faithful protection round his torso; the heavy insert plates giving a sense of security, sometimes invulnerability. He checked his radio and other equipment attached to the vest. He took the 9 mm Glock and checked the breech, slipped a full magazine into the handle and secured the weapon in the holster. He picked up the MP5 and checked and loaded the machine pistol carefully and efficiently. Leaving the cabin he walked out to join his team already waiting by the big armoured Landcruisers.

Thomas Hillman, was Jack's General Manager and second in command. They had served in the army together and been friends for over twenty years. He was a few years younger than Jack, slightly shorter and slimmer, with close cropped fair hair, tanned face and blue eyes. Born in the UK, he spent most of his younger life in Leeds. He had two daughters from a previous marriage, but his home now, was Dubai, where he lived with his wife, Helen. His passion was boats and he had spent more money than he, or Helen, had wished, on an old thirty foot yacht, which he sailed as often as possible when home.

Tom had spent several years with Military Intelligence, before meeting Jack. They had become friends, when they were thrown together on a mission with the UN Special Forces in Kosovo. Jack had been sent with a small detachment of SAS, to seek out and capture, or eliminate an Armenian warlord, who had been operating independently, on the Armenian, Kosovo border.

* * *

Dragan Vaslic, was a vicious thug, who controlled a small army of bandits, about two hundred strong. He had been targeting refugees, moving south into Armenia and was killing and robbing men women and children, with no regard for ethnicity or religion. Tom was assigned to Jack's team as intelligence liaison, reporting directly to his principles in the UN. They had parachuted into Kosovo, just over the border with Armenia and close to the last know location of Vaslic's army. The warlord was known to be a huge figure of a man, brutal and amoral. His preferred method of dispatching a victim was to beat them to death with a large hammer.

On the flight into the drop zone, Tom and Jack had discussed the mission and the actions they would take when, or if, they found Vaslic. It transpired they were both inclined not to undertake the capture option. They had the latest intelligence and once on the ground, had moved swiftly towards the valley most used by fleeing refugees. They had taken up a position in a small cave high up on the valley wall and spent two nights in the freezing cold, waiting for the bandits to show up.

On the third morning, just after daybreak, they heard the rumble of light armoured vehicles and trucks; from the south end of the valley. Within a few minutes the first vehicles came into view. At the head of the column was a big American 4x4, with two motorcycle escorts each side. The column stopped and a figure emerged from the lead vehicle. Through his powerful field glasses, Jack could see the figure was wearing a huge black fur coat and hat and looked more like a bear than a human. He handed the glasses to Tom, who confirmed this was their man. Tom had a small case with him in which he carried a high powered snipers rifle. He swiftly assembled the weapon and checked the magazine and scope. Meanwhile, Jack had called in the coordinates, giving an exact location of the bandit column. They knew once they opened fire, they would have a serious problem evading the small army below; the only option was to call in an airstrike.

Tom had assumed a prone position and settled himself, ready to take the shot. Vaslic had several of his cohorts around him and considering his gestures, arm waving and pointing, looked to be giving orders, on the day's intended killing spree. Tom waited until the warlord had finished his briefing and stood still to light a large cigar. He took careful aim and gently squeezed the trigger. Through his field glasses, Jack saw the blood spurt, as Tom's high powered bullet went through the warlord's head. With the death of their leader, the bandits took cover, then, and not knowing from where the shot had originated, began firing in all directions. Jack and his team kept their heads down and sensibly did not return fire. No more than five or six minutes had passed, when suddenly the valley floor below erupted in explosion and flame, as the two cruise missiles hit their target.

Five years later Jack left the military and joined Tom, in the private security business.

* * *

The second member of Jack's regular team was Santosh Nishaad. Born in Kerala, Southern India. He was wing man and driver of the second armoured vehicle. In his mid-thirties he had been in the Indian Army for several years before taking the Baghdad contract and had worked with Jack for almost four years. Tall with a pleasant face and a huge smile, he was very fit and pumped, due to his relentless training in the gym. He was an imposing figure with a heart like a lion when on the streets.

Ali Wassam, was an Iraqi local, raised in Baghdad and ex Republican Guard, now the rear gunner in the second Landcruiser. Ali would always do what was best for Ali, but was still a trusted member of the team. Short, stocky and built like a wrestler, he smiled very little and had worked with Jack for almost a year.

'Good morning, guys,' said Jack.

'Morning, boss,' replied Santosh.

'Morning, mate,' said Tom.

Ali's usual grunt constituted his morning pleasantry. Jack relied on these men, they worked as a team and each instinctively knew what the others were thinking when on the street. They respected, trusted and depended on each other. They began their short pre journey briefing, but the clatter of two low flying Blackhawks, made conversation impossible for a few seconds. They looked up and watched as the anti-rocket flares the choppers had deployed drifted down and burned out. The helicopters descended as they made their approach to the helipad in the centre of the Green Zone. The guys boarded their respective armoured vehicles,

'Radio Check,' said Jack into the mic at his throat.

'Copy,' from Ali in the second vehicle.

'Good to go,' from Santosh and the radio fell silent.

Jack started the powerful engine of the Landcruiser, flicked on several flashing warning lights, including the headlights and moved slowly out of the covered parking space, towards the gates of the compound. He checked the rear view and saw the second vehicle a few metres behind, headlights and warning lights flashing as usual. The security guard at the gate opened it and saluted as the vehicles drove through.

They drove slowly within the Green Zone, and made their way to Checkpoint 12, one of the main entry and exit checkpoints which secured the Green Zone from the rest of Baghdad city; the Red Zone. As they approached CP 12 they slowed to a crawl in order the American sentries could recognize they were Brits. The small, proudly displayed Union Jack in the corner of the windscreen prompted the sentries to wave them through with a cursory thumbs-up. The vehicles negotiated the chicane of concrete barriers and exited the checkpoint slowly. The radio from the second vehicle crackled,

'Good to go.'

Which prompted a 'Rock & roll,' from Jack.

The vehicles surged forward as the accelerator pedals were pushed hard to the floor. They sped away from the killing area just outside the checkpoint and within a few seconds were heading towards Route Irish, the code name for the main highway to BIAP, the Baghdad International Airport.

Chapter Five
'Sadr City'

Route Irish was as busy as usual at this time of the morning, with locals using this main route through the city. The six lane highway was divided by a wide landscaped central reservation, resplendent with mature palm trees and lush colourful foliage. The twelve kilometre section from the Green Zone to the airport had several slip-roads joining and leaving the highway. Several bridges crossed the road and always presented a concern, as they offered opportunity to fire down onto on-coming military convoys and individual security vehicles. Castle's two Landcruisers did not waste time traversing Route Irish and it was the norm to travel in excess of one hundred and forty kliks along this dangerous section of road. With all lights flashing and, when needed, sirens blaring, the Landcruisers cut their way through the busy traffic, which swiftly parted to allow the big vehicles to pass unhindered.

There was no chatter between the team, as all on board were focused on the task of reaching the airport safely. Only a potential threat would solicit the use of the radio. The journey was going well and the small convoy had reached the halfway point on the road. This area had three bridges crossing in quick succession, with on and off ramps making it an even more hazardous location. Jack concentrated on the high speed driving, while Tom scanned both sides of the road for possible threats. His attention was suddenly drawn to a large brown van parked on the second of the three bridges,

'Stationary vic on the centre overpass,' he called into the radio.

It was not normal to see vehicles parked on the bridges and there was clearly concern in Tom's voice. No sooner had he finished speaking than an RPG missile streamed from the open side of the suspect vehicle.

'Oh, fuck,' exclaimed Jack.

'Contact. Contact,' shouted Tom.

Jack hit the brakes and then swerved, luckily evading the imminent explosion. The missile hit the road about ten metres in front of them, the blinding flash and deep bang causing Jack to wince as he fought to control the big vehicle. The shockwave buffeted the AV as the explosion peppered the front radiator with shrapnel and concrete. Jack maintained control and accelerated away, heading for the off-ramp, his speed far too dangerous for the incline under normal circumstances, but at this stage his only concern was to clear the area, not an RTA.

Tom looked behind and saw the rear AV had managed to safely manoeuvre their vehicle onto the off-ramp in a more controlled manner than the first.

'The boys are clear and right behind us,' he confirmed, 'Nice driving, mate.'

They grinned at each other, but the sweat glistening on their faces confirmed their true emotions. They were out of the kill zone and moving along a smaller 'A' road that ran at right angles to the main highway. Tom was in communication with guys in the rear.

'Shit,' said Santosh, 'That was too fucking close.'

'Baastuds,' shouted Ali.

Tom and Jack grinned at the Iraqi's pronunciation. While the chatter between the two AV's was heated, it remained controlled. Jack glanced briefly at Tom again and both, out of pure relief, burst into laughter. They looked to the road in front and immediately stopped laughing when they saw the over-road sign indicating they were heading towards Sadr City.

Sadr is an old district of Baghdad and the main stronghold of the Mahdi Army, the main insurgent militia in Iraq. This area is virtually a no-go zone for the security forces and the guys knew this; they needed to get back to Route Irish as fast as possible. The central reservation kerb was far too high to jump, even for the big wheels of the Landcruiser, so the only option was to take a side road off and work back to the main road that way. They were looking for an option when the road in front was suddenly blocked by an old water tanker that had turned sideways.

'What the fuck is this shit?' said Tom

'Looks like we're being set up,' replied Jack.

It was evident to them both this was no accident, the RPG forcing them off the highway, now the tanker blocking their progress. They were being forced to take the next off road and into the tiny streets of Sadr. The situation was worsening by the second and could deteriorate into a firefight at any moment, it was not a matter of if, but when that would happen.

Jack swiftly flipped on the indicators to turn off the road,

'We can't go in here, boss,' said Santosh, a clear concern in his voice.

'We got no choice,' replied Tom, 'The road ahead is blocked.'

The four of them were calm, but knew their situation was serious. There was always a way out of any situation, but what they did not want to have to do in this part of the city was stand and fight; the only safe option was to drive out as soon and as fast as possible. Jack hit the brakes and turned hard right off the road, down the incline and into the narrow streets of the old city, looking in all directions for a way to get back to Irish. He and Tom had been in this part of Baghdad before and the streets, once off the main roads, were not much wider than one vehicle. Passing was difficult, with the big Landcruisers it was almost impossible.

'We're in the shit now, guys,' declared Tom.

'Fucking big time,' agreed Jack.

Buildings were close on each side of the narrow street and afforded anyone with the inclination good cover to shoot down onto the little convoy. There was no way to keep up speed now and they were driving at almost walking pace. They had now become prime targets. This was as bad as it could get. Whoever had fired the RPG and used the water tanker to block the road now had them on their home turf. The team knew their situation was critical and the silence over the radio confirmed this. The only positive element was the GPS tracker system in the vehicles. As soon as they deviated from the prearranged route (which was direct from Green Zone to the airport) a warning would have gone off in the company's operations room in the Green Zone. The guys in the ops room would now know the small convoy was in Sadr City and certainly in harm's way. The ops manager was already on the radio to Jack, establishing their situation.

As Tom concentrated on the rooftops, Jack weaved the vehicle through the tiny streets, constantly checking the rear mirror to confirm Santosh was keeping his AV close behind. They did not want to be split up in this neighbourhood. Ali had the rear gun port in the back door open and was ready for anything that came from behind. Jack swiftly briefed the ops manager of their position and concerns over what appeared to be a coordinated attack in order to force a small security convoy into Sadr.

'If they had just wanted to take us out they could have done so with the RPG on Irish,' he told the ops manager. As if to confirm Jack's conversation, the first rounds hit the top of the rear AV and bounced off the armoured roof. There was no need for Santosh to shout, 'Contact, contact,' as the rattle of the AK firing from the rooftop was evident. The next rounds thumped into the back of the rear vehicle and Ali clearly saw they were also under fire from a doorway about thirty metres away. The gun port in the back of the vehicle didn't have the angle for Ali to return fire to the roof, but that was not the case for the shooter at the doorway.

'Baastuds,' yelled Ali, as he opened up on the ground floor gunman. Jack and Tom saw the second rooftop assailant in front of them and his first rounds bounced off the bonnet and windscreen of their vehicle.

'Time to get the fuck outta here,' said Tom.

Jack was on the radio to the ops room advising his convoy was now under fire from multiple contacts and needed urgent support.

The only gun-port was in the back of the rear vehicle and Ali was returning fire to the street level attacker. If the rest of the team were to be effective, they would have to exit the vehicles and fight on foot; at this point that was not an option. Jack considered backing up and returning the way they had come, but decided it would not be beneficial. As he edged forward, he saw what looked to be a T junction about fifty metres ahead. They continued slowly towards the end of the street, as the shooters poured rounds onto the convoy. The sound of the AK's and the noise of the rounds beating down on the AV's armour was deafening. When they finally reached the end of the street, both Tom and Jack's hearts dropped; the narrow street to the left had been blocked by an old Toyota Pickup and to the right, the road was so small, a Landcruiser would not be able to get down it.

'Shit, we can't move forward guys,' said Jack into the throat mic. 'We'll have to reverse back'

'Roger that,' responded Santosh, as he put his vehicle into reverse.

He began to slowly move back just as Ali yelled, 'Stop stop!'

The spinning arc of a petrol bomb came off the rooftop above them, bursting onto the back of the rear vehicle, in a blinding yellow and crimson flame, setting fire to the outside of the Landcruiser .

'No facking way out now,' shouted Ali.

'Time to bailout,' declared Jack.

Just as they were about to exit the vehicles the shooting stopped. The thick acrid smoke from the rear fire drifted upwards in the still, cordite filled air. A door in the building in front of them opened and a crisp white table cloth, tied to a broom handle, in the manner of a 'flag of truce' came out. A second or two later the table cloth was followed by a man dressed in jeans and a red and whited checked keffiyah covering his head and face, sunglasses obscured his eyes. The strangest part of this vision, was the bright red Manchester United T-shirt the man wore. He stood for a few seconds, then shouted in good English,

'Get out of your vehicles and surrender, please.'

Jack and Tom looked at each other,

'Is he taking the piss?' said Tom.

'I like the please bit,' replied Jack sarcastically.

They both knew the only option now was to exit the vehicles and fight their way out on foot, being taken hostage was definitely not going to happen. Jack spoke calmly and clearly into the radio,

'We're bailing out guys, we'll have to fight our way to the main road on foot.'

'Yeah, fuck this shit, let's go,' came the reply from Santosh.

'Yeah let's get the fack out,' confirmed Ali.

They opened the left side doors of the vehicles and got out, but stayed behind the heavy shields the armoured doors offered. Jack could clearly see the street to the left went back to the road they had driven off, when the water tanker blocked their way. The road was only about a hundred metres away. If they could get to that, they would be out in the open and would stand a better chance than the rats-in-a-barrel situation they were in now. Manchester United shouted again, 'Please, drop your weapons and move away from your vehicles.' The clean white table cloth held high as he spoke. Tom had Man United in his sights, turning to Jack he said,

'Okay?'

Jack nodded, 'Yeah, do it.'

Tom gently squeezed the trigger on his MP5 and put three rounds into the United T shirt. The man was knocked off his feet and the flag of truce flew into the air, coming down over the lifeless body of the MU supporter, swiftly turning as red as the T shirt it covered.

Santosh and Ali joined Jack and Tom at the side of the lead vehicle, as theirs was now burning fiercely. With the killing of Man United; shooting from the rooftops in front, resumed in earnest. They were not taking any fire from behind, as the smoke and flame from the burning vehicle offered some cover. All four now turned their weapons on the rooftops. Jack turned to Santosh,

'Torch this fucker we're leaving nothing behind.'

Santosh smiled as he took a small pencil flare from a pouch on his body armour, ignited and tossed it onto the front seat of the lead vehicle, 'There goes a hundred and fifty grand,' he quipped.

They left the cover of the vehicle and moved smartly round the corner of the old building;
immediately drawing fire from two new shooters on the roof, as well as two more gunmen firing from the old Toyota pickup in front.

'We gotta take those bastards out,' shouted Jack.

'Yeah,' said Tom 'We get past that pickup and we're okay.'

Santosh and Ali were now firing at the shooters on the roof and doing a good job of keeping those guys' heads down. Tom and Jack fired on the pickup, as the four of them moved along the wall towards it. Shots came back and Tom was hit in the shoulder, the impact knocking him back against the wall.

'Ahhh for fuck sake,' he yelled.

The rooftop gunners had become more effective and one round caught Ali in the upper thigh, knocking him off his feet.

'Baastuds,' he screamed.

They took shelter in a deep doorway; Jack fired on the rooftop, Tom on the pickup, while Santosh quickly dressed the wound in Ali's leg, Ali cursed profusely in Arabic.

'Get a dressing on that shoulder, Tom,' said Jack.

'Fuck it,' came the adrenalin-fired response.

He was unable to use his left arm, but continued to fire on the pickup one handed. Santosh had finished dressing the leg and Ali was now back on his feet. Both had resumed fire on the roof shooters. The guys began moving along the wall towards the old Toyota; Tom and Jack's fire relentless. One of the pickup shooters seeing them so close, recklessly came out of cover and fired frantically at the four.

'Oh, thank you very much,' said Tom, as the man presented such an easy target.

He put several rounds into his torso, sending the attacker backwards against the side of the rusty old vehicle,

'Give that man a cigar,' quipped Jack.

The second shooter, not wanting to take these crazy guys on alone, abandoned his position and ran into one of the buildings. The four moved on past the bullet-riddled wreck, towards the open road, now only fifty metres away.

Running towards the road, Ali hung onto Santosh's body armour for support, moving as fast as he was able, cursing constantly; the bullet in his leg causing a lot of discomfort. There was no fire from the rooftops, but the pickup guy had re-joined the fight, along with two other shooters at street level. Jack surmised the rooftop shooters had come down to ground level to get a better shot at the escaping men. Tom was on point while Jack, Santosh and Ali returned fire to the rear. They stayed close to the wall and moved swiftly towards the end of the street, now only a few metres away. The road ahead was not busy, the few vehicles that were on it were moving very fast as the drivers heard the gunfire; no one wanted to get hit by a stray bullet.

'We need to get up this fucking banking and across the road,' shouted Tom, just as two new shooters opened up from the roof.

'We'll never make it with those bastards up there,' replied Jack.

It was going to be very dangerous to attempt a run up the banking and across the road now. The four continued to return fire to the rear and above, but they were quickly running out of ammunition for the MP5's, Ali had already run out and was using his 9 mil. Jack considered making a dash for the banking, but knew Ali would not be able to move fast enough, so dismissed the idea.

'Santosh and I will go for the road,' said Jack. 'Then we can cover you against those tossers on the roof. You up for it, buddy?' looking at Santosh.

'Okay with me, boss.'

The two were just about to break cover when the throaty rattle of a 30 calibre machinegun joined the cacophony. Seconds later a bloodied body fell from the roof with a splatter of blood and dust. More clatter from the 30 cal and then silence from the rooftops.

Tom looked around the corner of the building; fifty metres away and moving smartly along the elevated road was a Humvee, the rooftop gunner firing the heavy machine gun. Behind were three armoured Landcruisers from Jack's company.

'Oh, you fucking beauty!' said Tom.

The convoy moved forward, stopping about five metres away atop the banking. Half a dozen heavily armed men jumped from the front two armoured vehicles and quickly ran down the slope to support the four. 'Into the vehicles, *Now!*' shouted a burly Glaswegian. Jack and Santosh helped Ali up the banking. Tom, still looking over his shoulder followed behind, as the rescue team provided covering fire. No return fire came from the attackers who had obviously decided fighting a whole security convoy was not part of their game plan. The cover team returned to the AV's under the protection of the 30 calibre, as it continued to rake the narrow street. Tom's guys were unceremoniously bundled into the vehicles and a smart arse made the comments, 'Sadr City sightseeing is not recommended these days guys; you lot owe us a good drink for this.'

The convoy commander's voice came over the radios, 'Everyone in? All good to go?'

Several confirmations came from the four vehicles and the convoy began to reverse along the elevated road and moved back to the off-ramp, which Jack and his guys had been forced up thirty five minutes earlier. The line of vehicles expertly reversed down the ramp onto Route Irish, with no regard for the disturbance caused to oncoming local vehicles. Once the whole convoy had backed onto the motorway, they turned left and drove up onto the landscaped central reservation, cutting down various flowering shrubs and bushes as they crossed to the south bound carriageway. They would be back in the Green Zone in ten minutes.

Jack looked at Tom and asked, 'You okay, buddy, how's the shoulder?'

'It's fucking sore!'

A few seconds past, Jack turned to his friend again, 'You were okay taking Manchester United out, even though he had a white flag?'

Tom's face was stern. Then slowly a smile appeared, 'Yeah, no problem,' he grinned 'I'm a City supporter.'

Chapter Six
'The Map'

Four weeks after the Sadr City incident, Ali Wassam was still at home recuperating from the wound in his leg, but Tom was back from R&R in Dubai and had assumed light duties around the base. The wound in his shoulder had healed and according to his wife Helen, had left a sexy scar, but the muscle was still not a hundred percent.

Jack and the road crew were just arriving back into the covered parking area, after a short trip across the city. He saw Tom and waved, as he dismounted the big armoured vehicle, Tom walked over and said, 'Morning mate, good trip?'

'Hi, Tom,yeah no problems at all. How's the shoulder?'

'Getting better all the time,' Tom replied, as he spun his outstretched arm like a windmill.

'Okay good, don't be overdoing it, though.'

'Nah, its cool, I need to keep busy so I'm gonna strip out the old Kuwaiti Landcruiser and put some armour in the doors.'

'Okay sounds good. Need any help?'

'No thanks, I'm okay on my own.'

'Right. See you for lunch?'

'Sure.'

Jack slowly walked over to the accommodation area; the sun merciless in the clear blue sky. On entering his cabin, he went straight to the fridge and took out a can of Red Bull and quenched his thirst in three large gulps. He removed his body armour and securely stowed the weapons in the wall racks. Going into the bathroom, he washed the dust from his hands and face, removed the sweat soaked shirt and slipped on a clean one. His cellphone beeped and he checked the incoming text. It was on the intelligence network and had been sent out to all senior security personnel.

[urgent briefing/18:00 today/Republican Palace]

Jack replied to the message with a confirmation of his intention to attend.

Tom had moved the Kuwaiti Landcruiser from the parking area to the maintenance facility and had begun working on the secondary armouring of the vehicle. He had inserted Kevlar bags filled with sand into the cavities, in the driver's and off side passengers' doors and was in the process of removing the back door inside panel, when he noticed the plastic bottle wedged behind it. He removed the panel and recovered the bottle and wondered why anyone would stuff it in the door. He shook the bottle and the document inside rattled against the plastic. After trying unsuccessfully to remove it through the neck, he took out a knife and cut the bottle open. He spread the document out on the vehicle's bonnet and was intrigued to discover it was a map of Iraq and Northern Kuwait. *What the hell is this?* he thought to himself. He took his cellphone out and called Jack.

'Hi, Tom,' came the immediate response.

'You in your cabin mate?'

'Yeah, what's up?'

'I'll be there in a minute or two.'

'Okay.' The phone went dead.

He rolled up the map and walked over to the accommodation. Jack stood in the open doorway of his cabin. As his friend approached, he said, 'Everything okay, Tom?'

'Might have something interesting,' replied Tom, as he waved the rolled-up map.

He walked up the steps, kicked his boots against the top one, to get rid of the sand and went inside.

'You want a drink?'

'Cheers, yes, water please.'

Jack took two bottles from the fridge and they both sat down.

'Do you remember where we picked up that old Kuwaiti Landcruiser?' said Tom.

'Yeah, it's one of the local cars we bought when we got here in 2003. It's probably one of the vehicles that the Iraqi's stole from Kuwait when they bailed out in 91.

It's pretty knackered now, but it was top of the range back then.'

Tom stood up and spread the map out on the desk, 'I found this stuffed in a water bottle and hidden in the back door of it. Who would do that?'

'Who? is not the right question,' said Jack, putting on his glasses. 'Why anyone would hide it, is the right one. It's clearly Iraq and Northern Kuwait, but my Arabic is not good enough to read it, especially this hand written stuff,' said Jack, as he tapped the notation. He picked up his cellphone.

'Santosh?'

'Yes, boss.'

'Can you come to my cabin please?'

'Be right there, boss'

A few minutes later there was a knock on the door.

'Come in,' shouted Jack.

'What's up, boss?'

'Need you to translate this,' said Tom indicating the map.

Santosh leaned over the map and then said, 'It's a Republican Guard issue, 1991 series, Iraq and North Kuwait.'

'What about this?' said Tom, pointing to the written notation.

'It's a map reference, but I don't understand the rest.'

'What's it say, son?' said Jack.

'I think it says, *the best picnic in the world*,' said Santosh, a look of concentration on his face.

'Okay, cheers, buddy, that's all for now, see you later,' said Jack, patting him on the back.

'So, what'd you think?' said Tom, after Santosh had gone.

'I think it's an old map that someone stuck in the back door years, ago and it means nothing now.' said Jack.

'This is a Republican Guard map, issued in 91,' continued Tom, 'from when the Iraqis invaded Kuwait. The hand written map reference, could mean there's something important at that location, but this shit about a 'picnic' what's that all about?'

Jack got up and switched the kettle on, 'You want a coffee?'

'Just water, please.'

Jack made his coffee and sat down. 'Just a minute, I remember something I heard in 2003. Remember when we first arrived, we were billeted in the Flowerlands Hotel?'

'Yes,' said Tom. 'A bit of a shit hole really. We all had food poisoning at one time or another!'

'Yeah, that's right,' said Jack with a grimace, 'Imodium for breakfast. Anyway, there was a bunch of journalist staying at the hotel, across the road.'

'Yes, that's right, a real bunch of nosey bastards.'

'I remember talking to one from The Washington Post, Lisa Reynard. After a couple of   hours chatting, she gets round to telling me a story she'd heard from a CIA contact; about an Iraqi colonel who had looted a shit load of diamonds and then hidden them in a couple of picnic boxes in the desert.'

'That's a bit tenuous,' said Tom.

'Yes but I believed her. She was pissed by the end of the night and was coming onto me a bit.'

'Oh yeah?' said Tom with a grin.

'Yes she was a rather worse for wear; I ended up taking her to her room and putting her to bed.'

'So you just put her to bed and left?' again the grin.

'Yes. As I said, she was pissed, but the CIA and the colonel's story always stuck in my mind. She was so intent on about telling me the tale, it had to true.'

'Can you get in touch with her?'

'Yeah, I still have her contact details in the database, hold on.' He went to his laptop and a few minutes later said, 'Yeah, here she is, I'll email her and see if we can get a Skype chat, get more info. What you think?'

'Sure, why not?'

Jack quickly drafted a short mail and fired it off. 'Right, let's get some lunch.'

The 'incoming' alarm sounded as they left the cabin. 'Shit,' they said in unison and sprinted across the small compound and into the concrete bunker, just as the mortar exploded. A few moments later the second and third mortars exploded almost in unison. The explosions had not been far from their compound, but far enough away to have no impact other than terror. Jack fought to hold down the vomit rising in his throat, as he struggled to overcome the fear that gripped him; he did not want his friend to see the distress he was under. The 'all-clear' siren sounded and they left the bunker and continued their walk over to the dining facility.

'That's about thirty incoming, in the last week,' said Tom.

'Yeah, I'd rather be getting shot at on the road, than stuck in here waiting for those fucking mortars to land,' Jack mumbled. Regaining his composure he chuckled and said, 'Almost put me off me lunch.'

The acrid plumes of smoke could be seen about five hundred metres away, over towards the Green Zone's helipad, rising like three huge black genies. The wail of the emergency services' sirens were an unpleasant reminder that someone had been hurt, or worse. *Nowhere is safe in this bloody country,* thought Jack.

Chapter Seven
'Meetings'

Tom and Jack flashed their US Department of Defence IDs and the American sentry waved them through to the Republican Palace car park. They parked the vehicle under a tree to afford some shade and walked across to the main gates of the palace. At the large gatehouse they joined the queue of other non-military contractors and diplomats entering the imposing building. Security was stringent, but swift. After signing the log book, they exchanged their Department of Defence badges for clip-on visitor cards, which they duly attached to their shirts. The Republican Palace used to be Saddam Hussein's main residence, the largest, most elaborate and ostentatious of all the Baghdad palaces, but now it housed the US Military High Command and Provisional Government. The beautiful gardens with their fountains and statues reminded Jack of the time he'd visited the Palace of Versailles with Nicole. The memory prompted a smile and solicited the question from Tom, 'What you grinning about?'

'Just had a flashback, buddy, just a flashback,' he replied, as he patted Tom on the back.

They walked under the huge portico and entered the Grand Foyer of the palace. Jack had been here many times over the last five years and had never failed to be amazed at the opulence. The foyer was more the size of a large ballroom than an entrance. The white marble floor and walls shimmered in the reflected light of the biggest chandelier he had ever seen. A dozen golden columns supported the huge domed ceiling and between each column stood oversized 'Rodinesque' statues of Gods and warriors, but on closer inspection each statue had the face of Saddam Hussein. Tom looked at his friend and said, 'What a dump.'

'Yeah, a real shit hole,' laughed Jack.

They headed to the main briefing room and took a seat with the other contract security personnel. The big room was noisy and packed with about a hundred people, mostly men, with a sprinkling of women. All were dressed in para military uniforms, most wore baseball caps, some still wore their sunglasses.

A big sergeant at the front shouted, 'Stand please,' and the room went silent, as everyone got to their feet. A colonel stepped onto the low podium and spoke into a hand held microphone. 'As you were, gentlemen,' then noticing the few females he added, 'And ladies.'

A ripple of laughter went round the room and then silence as the colonel began his briefing.

* * *

Across the city in Mansour district, another meeting was about to take place. Ali Wassam took an outside table at the busy café and ordered two teas. A few minutes later the waiter returned and placed two small glasses of tea on small ornate saucers in front of Ali.

'Shukran,' he thanked the waiter, who nodded politely and returned inside. He put sugar in his tea, and stirred the drink slowly, watching the sugar dissolve. Ali then took the other teaspoon and formed an X with both spoons on the table. He was very nervous about the meeting; the stranger who had come to his home and instructed him to be here, frightened him. He had been given a scrap of paper with the name of the café, the address and a day and time to be there. The note also gave instructions on how the spoons were to be placed.

The temperature at this time of day was still over thirty centigrade, but it was anxiety, not heat, that caused the sweat to trickle down his back. His thoughts were of the man who had brought the note. 'Someone will meet you here,' the stranger had said, as the note was handed over. Ali read the simple instructions, then said, 'What is this about and who are you?'

'Just go to the meeting,' said the stranger, as he looked Ali straight in the eyes. 'If you do not, your wife will be raped and beheaded in front of you.' An involuntary shiver went through Ali's body; in his heart, he felt the stranger meant every word.

He was startled from his thoughts as a tall man cast a shadow over the table. Ali squinted in the evening sunlight; the man's face was in shade, but he could tell it was not the same person who had come to his home. The stranger sat down and picked up one of the crossed spoons, turning it over and over in his fingers, then said, 'Salaam Alaikum, you are, Ali Wassam?'

'Alaikum Salaam. Yes, I am Ali.'

The man was about thirty years old and looked very fit. He wore sandals, black jeans and black tee-shirt, with a black keffiyah wrapped around the top of his head. His face was tanned and his thick black beard neatly trimmed. His eyes were hidden behind what looked like Ray Bans, but the spelling in the corner of the lens said *Ray Bon*.

'What do you want with me?' said Ali, as he tried to keep the fear from his voice.

'I will get to that in due course, brother,' said the stranger, 'But needless to say we have several tasks for you to undertake.'

'Who are we?' said Ali, as calmly as he could.

'*We* are the men who will bring the true faith to the world; *We* are the Islamic State of Iraq and the Levant.'

* * *

The meeting in the Republican Palace had finished and the attendees milled out of the sumptuous hall and into the Grand Foyer. 'Let's go get some dinner here,' suggested Jack.

'It's the best grub in Iraq,' replied Tom, 'Why not?'

The opulent dining hall was packed with about four hundred people, mostly military, but interspersed with government people and senior subcontractors. They joined the queue at the service counter and were quickly served with a large steak, french fries and salad. After picking up a couple of cans of Red Bull from the chiller, they began looking for a table and found two seats on a table with six burly marines.

'May we join you, gentlemen?' said Tom.

'Yes, sir,' replied the nearest soldier, as he moved his plate slightly to make more room.

The marines joked and laughed among themselves and were clearly in good spirits. Tom and Jack ate their meal leisurely and spoke quietly. 'What do you think of the briefing?' said Tom. Jack finished a mouthful of steak and then answered, 'I've heard of this 'ISIL' before. It was a couple of years ago when they took over parts of Syria. But that place is a clusterfuck, so anyone could get a foothold there. I can't see the same happening in Iraq, no way.'

'That's what I think, mate,' replied Tom. 'But this new intelligence is saying otherwise, so as far as I'm concerned it's just more shit for us to have to deal with.'

'Yeah,' said Jack, 'You finished?'

'Yes, let's split.'

They both stood and Jack said to the marines, 'You guys be safe.'

'Always,' came the reply

Jack helped himself to another Red Bull from the chiller, as they were leaving the dining room. They walked along the extravagantly decorated Golden Hallway, back to the Grand Foyer and out into the warm evening air. They joined the queue at the main gatehouse, exchanged the visitors' cards for their DoD badges, collected the vehicle from the car park and were back in their own compound ten minutes later. They parked the vehicle under the shaded area and Jack said, 'I need a shower.'

'Me too,' replied Tom. 'See you later?'

'Yep, will do.'

Jack entered his cabin and checked the laptop. He noticed the reply from Lisa Reynard saying she would be available for a Skype conference the following morning at 08:00 Eastern Standard Time.

'Great,' he said out loud.

After showering, he switched on Skype and called Nicole. They had met in Russia, fifteen years earlier and had been together ever since. Nicole had been a model and her father, Dimitri had hired him to 'mind' her while she was working in Moscow. Her father was a true

Russian oligarch, in every sense of the word, with interests in oil, mining and steel. He also had several lucrative properties in London and New York and as a hobby, owned a major football club in the UK. But his pride and joy was his prestigious golf club in Scotland, of which he was the majority shareholder. Nicole's mother had been English and had died when Nicole was very young. She was now thirty-eight and a successful business woman in her own right, with a chain of health spas in the UK, as well as an impressive portfolio of London properties.

'Hi, darling,' she said, as the Skype camera showed her face.

'Hi, Nikki, how are doing? What you up to?'

'I'm fine, darling. I'm in Manchester, for the opening of the new spa.'

'Oh, good how's that going? Everything under control?'

'All good, we'll be open on time and Daddy's got a few of his soccer player friends to send their wives along.'

'Great, so you're in with the 'Cheshire wives' from the start. Well done.'

'What you up to, Jack? Why you calling this time of day? Is everything all right?'

'I'm fine, darling. Nothing to worry about, but we may have stumbled onto something big. We might be off the grid for a few days; we'll be heading into the desert, but nothing for you to worry about.'

'You sure?'

'Yeah, promise, I'll give you a call before we set off. Soon as we're back I'll be in touch. Don't worry.'

'Okay. Talk soon, darling. Love you lots. Be safe.'

'I will. Love you too. Bye, darling,'

Chapter Eight
'Millionaires'

The following morning Jack was at his laptop and had just switched on Skype, when there was a knock on the door.

'Come in.'

Tom came in and went straight to the fridge. As he helped himself to a bottle of water he said, 'Are we all set for the Skype conference?'

'Yeah, a couple'o minutes and she should be online'.

No sooner had he finished speaking than the laptop buzzed, indicating an incoming call. Jack clicked on the icon and a moment later the screen showed Lisa Reynard.

'Hi there,' she said with a smile. 'Long time, no hear. How're you guys doing over there?'

Lisa was in her late thirties, tanned face, brown eyes and long dark blonde hair; her accent was upmarket New York. She was a successful journalist, photographer and writer and had been working in the Washington Post's Baghdad bureau when Jack had met her in 2003.

'Hello, Lisa, good to talk to you again. We're okay, still a hellhole,' Jack laughed. 'I have, Tom Hillman here with me. You remember, Tom?'

Tom moved into view of the camera and his face appeared on screen, 'Hello again, Lisa.'

'Yes, I remember, Tom. Hi there, honey.'

Tom sat down again out of camera view.

'This is all very mysterious guys. What's it about? You got a story for me?'

'Actually, Lisa we need a story from you,' said Jack

'Okay, go ahead, honey.' She put her elbows on the desk and leaned closer to the screen.

'Right,' Jack began, 'Back in 2003, you told me a tale about some diamonds that had been looted by an Iraqi colonel.'

'Yes, I do remember,' she interrupted. 'It seemed like a great story at the time, but just slipped away to nothing.'

'Could you tell us again please?' said Jack.

She sat back in her chair and looked at the ceiling, as the details came back to her.

'I got the story from an old friend in the CIA. He told me about an Iraqi colonel who had been found in a crashed vehicle. It was back in 91, when the Iraqi's were high-tailing it out of Kuwait and retreating to Baghdad. He had suffered a head injury and had subsequently died during interrogation.'

'Yeah, but what about the diamonds? You talked about a load of looted diamonds,' Jack said.

'That's right,' she continued. 'The colonel had a handful of stones on him when he was found. He told his interrogators he'd hidden the diamonds in a couple of picnic boxes, somewhere in the desert; the location had been marked on a map. But he died before he could tell them where the map was.' She stopped talking and leaned into the screen again. 'But I know where the map is,' she said. 'You guys have it!'

Jack held the map up to the camera and nodded. 'Oh how wonderful,' said Lisa.

'Any idea how much the stones are worth?' said Jack.

'I don't know what the value is, but my contact said the colonel reckoned he had taken about twenty kilos, which is a lot. Just a second, let me Google it.' After a few seconds she exclaimed, 'I don't believe it.'

'How much, Lisa? How much?' insisted Jack.

'Oh my God, it's over a billion dollars!'

Jack and Tom immediately jumped up. Tom shouted, 'Jackpot,' linked arms with Jack and began dancing round the cabin.

Lisa laughed, then shouted over the mic. 'Hey, you guys, I want the story.'

They calmed down and Jack returned to the laptop, 'You can have the story, babe, but only after we find the diamonds and return them to the Kuwaitis.'

'Hold on a minute,' interrupted Tom, 'We're gonna give 'em back?'

'No, No. Not give them back. Return them for a substantial reward,' said Jack, 'We would never be able to dispose of that many diamonds without causing ourselves a shit load of agro, but if we return them we get a legitimate reward.'

'And a lot of publicity,' said Lisa. 'There's a big story here, guys.'

'Okay, Lisa, thanks for your help. We'll let you know how we get on.'

'Look forward to talking again soon, guys.'

'Oh, and, Lisa, you gotta keep this under wraps for now.'

'Sure sweetie, no problem.'

'There'll be a story and a share for you, when it's all over.'

'Ooh goody, I could do with some new Jimmy Choo's. Bye, guys, be safe. Good luck.'

'Bye.' said Jack and Tom in unison. The screen went blank and Jack closed the laptop. Tom stood up, took two bottles of water from the fridge and handed one to Jack.

'You've got a plan already,' said Tom, with a grin.

'Yeah, but we need to get the guys together first,' replied Jack.

'Who've you got in mind, mate?'

'You, me, Danny and Steve.'

'Ian as well?' added Tom.

'Yep, Ian as well, plus Santosh and Ali Wassam, seven of us in three vehicles.'

They both stood, grinned at each other and after a celebratory hug, Tom said, 'I'll contact the guys and get them together as soon as possible. Steve has to come down from Tikrit, by chopper; soon as we know when he can get here, we can get the rest of the lads in.'

'Okay, cheers, buddy.'

Tom opened the door and was about to leave when Jack shouted, 'Hey.'

'Yes?'

'This time next year, Rodney, we'll be millionaires.'

Tom laughed out loud, as he closed the door.

Chapter Nine
'The Old Iraqi'

The builders' market was bustling with people, selling and buying everything to do with construction, from old rusty screws to heavy equipment. Santosh Nishad had been sent to purchase breeze blocks, to build a small wall next to the covered parking area on Castle's compound. He was bartering with a local trader, who was not moving from five dollars each, when an old Iraqi man had pulled at his sleeve, 'Salam,' said Santosh, as he smiled at the old guy.

'I have blocks for sale, sir.'

'How much and how many?' said Santosh.

'About a hundred, sir and only one dollar each.'

The local trader waved his hands and shouted to the interloper to go away, but Santosh had taken the old man by the arm and moved him away from the now belligerent seller.

'Deliver them to this compound in the Green Zone, soon as you can please,' instructed Santosh.

'Thank you, sir,' replied the old man; clearly delighted he had made the sale.

'My name and company are on this paper.'

* * *

The old Iraqi had returned to the shanty that served as his home. The olive grove close by not only offered shade during the day, but produced ripe fruit in the summer months and firewood in the winter. Looking through the clump of trees the old man had found five strong branches that would serve as 'supports' and after an hour of cutting, had dragged the timbers back to his home.

His breathing was shallow and laboured with the exertion and the heat did nothing to help his condition. Taking the wood inside the shack he skilfully inserted the stout branches into place, securely supporting the roof of the tiny ramshackle building. After resting for a while, he began the arduous process of dismantling the one wall that was made from un-cemented breeze blocks. Wheezing and moving slowly, he piled them into the back of the rusty pickup he'd borrowed. With sweat stinging his eyes, he sipped from his last bottle of water. He prayed the Indian in the Green Zone would take them, even though they were not new. He needed the money and the thought of a hundred dollars to buy food, made the heavy work bearable.

The old man then set about securing the large opening in the side of his home, with the few corrugated sheets he had found, fastening them to the branches with various lengths of wire and rope. He had also collected several cardboard boxes and after filling them with sand

and stacking them on top of each other, was able to close up the remaining gap. Standing back and surveying his work, he was confident the replacement wall would keep out some of the heat, if not the dust. After loading the last remaining blocks onto the old truck, he nodded to himself, satisfied with his day's work. He was now ready to be at the entrance to the Green Zone by 6am the following morning.

* * *

The old man had been waiting for two hours in the rusty pickup. With no air-conditioning and the hot sun beating down on the dented roof, he was struggling to stay alert. The salty sweat stung his eyes, as he wiped his face with a dirty rag. The burning thirst had not been quenched by the last few drops of his water and there were still half a dozen vehicles to be checked before he could get into the Green Zone.

An hour later the old pickup arrived at the gate to Castle's compound. Santosh's cellphone beeped, 'Yep?'

'Mr Santosh, sir?'

'Yes.'

'This is the gate sir. There's an Iraqi here with a delivery of breeze blocks and he's asking for you.'

'Okay no problem I'll be there in a couple of minutes.'

Santosh parked his vehicle at the side of the gate house, the dust causing the young Indian guard to cough and splutter.

'Is he clear to come in?' he said the guard.

'Yes, sir, him and truck both checked,' said the guard wanting to show his efficiency.

'TeKay,' replied Santosh, using the Indian colloquialism.

He walked over to the old man and shook his hand, 'Salaam Alaikum.'

'Alaikum Salaam,' replied the old man, 'Can you give me water please, sir?'

'Sure. Hey, bring me a bottle of water,' he shouted to the guard.

The sentry almost fell over the guardhouse step, in his haste to do as he had been ordered. Quickly returning with the water, he handed it to Santosh, who passed it to the Iraqi.

'Shukran, sidi. Thank you.'

The old man took a few sips of the water, replaced the top and put the bottle in his cab. Santosh smiled and said, 'Okay, follow my truck please.' The old man climbed into his cab and slowly drove forward through the gate. A few minutes later they both arrived at the covered parking area. 'Hold on and I'll get someone to unload the blocks,' said Santosh.

A few minutes after calling the maintenance office two young Asian maintenance guys arrived.

'Get this lot unloaded,' he snapped.

The old man took his water and sat on the ground, his back against the front wheel of the pickup, the welcome shade and cool water reviving him a little. The Indian gentleman had not said anything about the blocks not being new and the fact they were being un-loaded meant he was going to keep them. He smiled to himself at the thought of the hundred dollars. He had not eaten anything substantial for three days, but tonight he would fill his belly and thank God for the Indian.

Santosh was supervising the unloading when Tom Hillman drove up in the old Kuwaiti Landcruiser. Parking under the shade, next to the battered rusty pickup, he said to Santosh,

'Hi buddy, how you doin?'

'Okay, boss.'

The old man stood up and politely nodded to the Westerner, 'Salaam sidi.'

'Salaam,' replied Tom.

The door to the Landcruiser was open and Tom noticed the old man's face suddenly become transfixed. The old guy appeared to have become startled by the large dark stains on the driver's seat and door. The Iraqi gave a deep moan and slowly sank to his knees, he mumbled something in Arabic, then dropped the plastic bottle. The water ran out and soaked into the hot sand. The old man fell to the ground, his mouth open, as he gasped for breath.

'Call the medic,' Tom shouted to Santosh.

* * *

The old man woke, his breathing easier, thanks to the gentle supply of oxygen being delivered through the mask over his mouth and nose. He lay on a bed, in a cool clean room that smelt of disinfectant. Another Westerner was leaning over him and noting he had regained consciousness said, 'My name is Ian, I'm a medic. How you feeling, wee man?'

The mask was removed and the Iraqi said, 'I don't feel good, sir.'

Tom and Jack stood at the other side of the bed watching Ian check the old boy's pulse and blood pressure. After making sure the mask was back in place, Ian turned to them and quietly said, 'He's nae in good shape, guys.'

The man took the mask from his face and began to speak slowly, first in Arabic and then even slower in English, 'The white truck, the white truck with the marks on seat and door.'

'What's he on about?' said Ian.

'He means the old Kuwaiti Landcruiser,' said Tom.

'He means the stains on the seat and door, we've never managed to get em out,' said Jack.

The Iraqi was talking again between gulps from the oxygen mask. 'This is the truck I came to Baghdad with,' he gasped more oxygen. 'This is the truck I found in the desert many years ago.'

The old guy was drawing more oxygen from the mask now, his chest moving up and down, sweat on his forehead.

'He is nae good, guys. We need to let him rest,' insisted Ian.

'No, no, I must speak.' His breath rattled in his throat. 'My wife is dead, my son is dead, all because I brought my family to Baghdad in that cursed truck.'

Ian was holding his wrist and said, 'His pulse is racing, we gotta let him calm down and rest.'

'No, I must make my peace with God.'

Ian dabbed a water soaked sponge stick against the old man's lips.

'My son was taken from me, he became involved with crazy young men,' he gulped the oxygen deeply.

'A few weeks ago I was told he had martyred himself in a market car bomb.' A pitiful moan came from deep inside him and tears rolled down his cheeks.

'He did not only martyr himself, his mother, my wife, was in the market that morning.'

The tears filled his eyes and he wiped them away with his calloused fingers.

'She was killed in the market that morning, my beautiful wife died with my son.'

The old man's chest heaved and his eyes, wide open, stared at the ceiling,

'I will be with you soon, Nabila, Allah O Akbah.'

His body went limp; Ian quickly checked his pulse again and said, 'The old boy's gone.'

Chapter Ten
'Arrivals'

The smell from the barbecue filled the air and the bitter sweet aroma of rich barbecue sauce permeated the compound. Daniel Chaplain flipped large T bone steaks and great slabs of ribs on the oversized fire pit, which in a previous life had been an oil drum, now chopped in half, with a grill large enough to accommodate several man-size pieces of meat at once.

Daniel was in his late forties, with close cropped brown hair and brown eyes. Occasionally, if the weather was cold, he walked with a slight limp, from a wound he had sustained at Goose Green during the Falklands conflict. Born in Newcastle he was a proud Geordie with an accent that sometimes needed subtitles, a strong family man with two teenage sons; everyone called him Danny, unless they were taking the piss and then he got Daniel.

'Any chance we can eat sometime this week, Daniel?' joked Tom.

Laughter in the group as Ian added, 'He's fucking useless.'

'You lazy bastards can do it yourselves, now get t'fuck', replied Danny indignantly.

The banter and good humour continued and Danny remained the brunt of their jibes as he worked away on the grill. Jack passed out cans of beer from a large cool box filled with ice, giving the odd one a shake before handing it over. Ian opened his beer and the spurt from the can caught him square in the eyes,

'Oh, ya bastard,' he shouted, as he wiped the foam from his face.

Ian Andrew Little was the medic. Born in Edinburgh and a young-looking forty, he was tall with black hair and dark eyes, always immaculately turned out, with a cutting sense of humour; he was unmarried and had a gay partner back home in Scotland.

Jack, Tom, Santosh and Ian were sitting round the fire as Danny handed out the plates, the large slabs of meat hanging over the edges and thick dark sauce dripping onto the sand.

'Cheers, pal,' said Ian as he licked the sauce from the back of his hand, 'This looks great.'

'Thanks, boss,' said Santosh, as he lifted the plate to his nose inhaling the aroma.

After passing Jack and Tom their plates Danny joined the circle around the fire, sat down and opened a can of beer. Raising it to no one in particular, he said, 'Cheers, guys, it's good to be here. Bon appy tit.'

A sandstorm earlier in the day had delayed Steve, so Jack decided not to talk about the plan until everyone was present. Soon as Steve arrived, he would bring in Ali and go through the story and plan to recover the diamonds. Tom knew his friend was thinking about the stones and what needed to be done to get their 'reward'; he leaned over to Jack and said, 'Chill out mate, the plan is good, we've everything covered, relax tonight.'

'Yeah you're right, cheers, buddy.' Jack tapped his can of Coke against his friend's beer can.

The wailing sound of the 'incoming' alarm brought them swiftly to their feet and, with plates and beer in hand, they dashed to the nearby bunker and crowded in. Jack was last under the thick concrete roof, just as the mortar detonated. Automatically he said, 'Everyone in?'

'All in, boss,' came the reply.

The second explosion caused Jack to wince and the nausea to build in his throat. It had never got any easier for him, even after five years of sheltering in these fucking bunkers; every time the mortars came in, his fear manifested and the only thing he could do was hold down the desire to vomit and wait for the 'all-clear'. The guys were now sitting on the floor cross legged and tucking into their steaks, as the third and fourth explosions reverberated through the Green Zone.

'Just another wee night in Ol' Baghdad,' quipped Ian and the five burst into laughter.

* * *

The central helipad for all military flight movements is located in the middle of the Green Zone; an extremely well protected location with four metre high blast walls and stringent security. Access to this area was for military personnel and Department of Defence badge holders only.

Jack had left his vehicle in the nearby parking area and walked across the road to the main entrance checkpoint. The American soldier in the gatehouse saluted and said, 'Are you travelling, sir?'

'Pick up only today.'

'ID please, sir.'

Jack handed over his DoD badge and the soldier scanned it efficiently. Passing it back, he noticed the blue stripe across the top of the card, denoting the highest level of clearance for civilian personnel. He saluted again, 'Very good, sir. Please follow the signs for Arrivals.'

'Thank you.'

'Have a safe day, sir.'

Jack entered the small Arrivals building, went over to the fridge and helped himself to a bottle of water. He checked the monitors for arrival times of incoming choppers and their departure locations. The place was busy, as most flights had been grounded the day before due to the sand storm. He had been given a ball-park time of arrival for Steve, but flight information here was only a guide; helicopters frequently deviated from their normal flight plans, due to fluid operational requirements and, of course, ground attack from small arms and RPGs. Steve was due in at midday, direct from Tikrit and according to the monitors, his flight was 'on-time'.

'Hello there,' said Geoff Mason, as he patted Jack on the back.

Castle turned and smiled, extended his arm and the two men shook hands.

'Hey, Geoff, how ya doing buddy?'

'I'm good, Jack. How's business?'

'It's good, its good,' nodded Jack.

'I heard you had a bit of a problem in Sadr City a few weeks ago, everyone okay?'

'Yeah, we let ourselves get pulled into an ambush. Bad judgment on my part.'

'I doubt that, Jack,' said Geoff, with a frown on his face. 'But everyone's okay?'

'Couple a guys wounded, nothing that won't heal. You waiting for your guys to come in?'

'No. I'm picking up the Italian Ambassador; he's coming down on the shuttle from the airport.'

'Nice, how's the grub over at the embassy these days?

'Yeah, it's pretty good. You and Tom should come over the next time there's a party.'

'Sounds cool. Just let us know.'

'Will do. Okay here's my man now, see you soon, Jack, be safe eh.'

They shook hands.

'You too , Geoff.'

Steve Shelby was born and raised in London, until he joined the army at sixteen. A couple of years younger than Jack, he was an imposing figure, tall and muscular; who used his physique to his advantage, when playing rugby for his regiment. Steve and Danny were friends who had met and served together in the Falklands. Steve had lost an eye at Goose Green, while rescuing Danny from an exposed outcrop. Steve always played down the rescue of his friend, but Jack remembered the story Danny had told him.

* * *

They had landed with the rest of the 2nd Parachute Regiment, at San Carlos Water and had moved down the island under the command of the now famed, Colonel 'H' Jones; who was subsequently killed during the action. Their orders were to assault and if possible capture, Goose Green. The Argentinians were entrenched on the summit of Darwin Hill and the Para's came under serious attack from mortar and machine gun fire, as they attempted to capture the strategic position.

Steve, a sergeant at the time, had been ordered to take seven paratroopers and neutralize a heavily fortified machine gun emplacement. Steve had split his team into two, four-man groups and planned to move on the emplacement from opposing angles. The terrain was low gorse and scrub, which offered virtually zero cover. Steve, with his three men, had moved within grenade throwing distance of the emplacement, by way of a water filled gulley. Danny, a corporal and in charge of the second team, had no such luck with cover and assaulted the emplacement with all four men, firing their automatic rifles, drawing fire from Steve. The Argentinians opened up on Danny's team and he was hit in the upper thigh, breaking his femur. One other trooper was hit in the shoulder and the four became pinned down, with nowhere to go.

Steve had broken cover and ran out to Danny and his beleaguered men. An Argentinian had hurled a grenade towards Steve; the explosion knocking him off his feet, as shrapnel hit him in the face. Adrenalin had kept him going and he'd dragged Danny from the field of fire, while his own team had kept the Arg'ies busy. Grenades, thrown by Steve's guys had taken out the gun emplacement and left the way clear for the rest of the company to move on up Darwin Hill and ultimately to capture Goose Green.

* * *

Normally he would have an artificial eye in place, but here in Iraq, the dust and sand irritated the dry socket, so Steve wore a rakish black eye patch; which along with his bald head, occasionally gave rise to various piss takers calling Blofeld! Steve had worked with Jack since 2003 and they had become close friends.

Steve came in through the Arrivals door, along with several marines and a couple of civilian security personnel.

'Afternoon, Steve.'

'Hey, boss, how you doing?' They shook hands and hugged, 'What's it all about?'

'I'm good and all will be revealed in due course. Patience, patience,' said Jack with a smile,

'Okay, let's get back to the compound.'

They left the building and, after having their ID cards scanned at the gatehouse, walked over to the carpark. Steve threw his small rucksacks and body armour into the back of the vehicle and climbed in. Jack moved out of the exit and onto the busy roadway. In less than ten minutes they were parking under the covered area on their compound. Tom saw them arrive and walked over to the vehicle. The usual hugs and greetings were exchanged, along with a few good humoured insults. Santosh arrived and the same greeting formalities were exchanged, but this time no insults were traded. 'Can you show Steve which cabin he's in please, Santosh?'

'Okay, boss.'

'Get settled in and we'll see you at my place in an hour.'

Steve looked at his watch and said, 'Sure, boss, see you then.' As he walked away he turned to Santosh, 'How you doing Santosh, how's the family?'

'I'm good, family all okay as well, boss.'

'Which cabin is Danny in?' continued Steve.

'He's next to you. He got here yesterday.'

As he entered his cabin, the cellphone beeped and not recognizing the number displayed, he said, 'Jack Castle, Security Op's.'

'Lisa Reynard, Washington Post,' came the cheery response.

'Lisa,' said Jack with surprise, 'How are you?'

'I'm good, sweetie. I need a lift.'

'What? Where are you?'

'I'm at the airport, just arrived from DC via Istanbul. Would you send someone to bring me to the Green Zone please?'

'What the hell are you doing here, Lisa?'

'Just send someone to pick me up, honey and I'll tell you when I get there.' The phone went dead. Jack turned to Tom and said, 'Get the vehicles ready, we've got an airport run.'

'What's the score?' said Tom.

'Lisa Reynard is at the bloody airport. We need to pick her up.'

Chapter Eleven
'Unexpected guest'

Before the invasion of Iraq the main airport in Baghdad was called Saddam International but, since the dictator's demise, had been renamed Baghdad International Airport, usually referred to as BIAP. It had been built in the 70s by a German consortium and, although efficient and substantial at that time, now struggled to cope. The huge amount of passenger and cargo traffic moving in and out since 2003 had effectively rendered it 'un-fit for purpose'.

The downstairs Arrivals area was packed with locals, pushing and shoving, excitedly waiting for friends and relatives to appear. Foreign support company reps collected dozens of Asian workers, marshalling them into neat rows; each with their tiny plastic carrier bags containing their worldly goods, The reps shouting and pushing them into line, ready to be marched off to waiting buses and their high paying jobs supporting the American military. Security escorts, each waving various printed name boards, pushed their way to the front of the crowd to seek out their 'charges' as quickly as possible. The lighting was poor at best and the air-conditioning struggled to cope with the exit doors constantly opening and an outside temperature of 40C. To say the smell was unpleasant would be a compliment but, despite the many negative elements, the old airport always had a sense of excitement about it.

Jack scanned the busy Arrivals hall, but could not see Lisa anywhere. He took out his cellphone and returned the call she had made to him.

'Jack,' came the immediate response, 'I'm upstairs in the bar,'

'See you in a few minutes,' he said.

'The bar?' said Tom.

'Yep,'

Lisa sat by the window and watched the planes land and take off, a half finished glass of beer on the table in front of her.

'Hi, Lisa,' said Jack, 'What the hell are you doing here?'

Born in New York, in her late-thirties, Lisa Reynard was tall and athletic, her olive skin and dark eyes a testament to her Italian heritage. She wore khaki trousers and a loose fitting khaki shirt, with well-worn desert boots. Her hair was secured by the rear clasp of a black baseball cap, her sunglasses rested on the peak. She had become a renowned photo-journalist with the Washington Post and had worked several conflict zones, over the last ten years.

'Great to see you again, Jack,' she said with a brilliant smile.

93

'Yeah, you too, I guess,' as he gave her a hug.

'Hi, Tom. How're you, honey?'

'I'm good, Lisa. Bit surprised to see you though!'

'Okay, let's get back to the Green Zone, and we'll talk about what the hell you think you're doing here,' chided Jack.

Tom picked up her small rucksack and camera bag and the three set off back to the parking area.

Santosh, Danny and Steve were waiting by the two Landcruisers. 'Oh very nice,' said Danny, when he saw Lisa coming towards them.

'Calm down, tiger,' said Steve, as he punched Danny in the shoulder.

'This is Lisa Reynard,' said Jack, as he introduced her to the three men in turn. 'She's gonna be with us for a few days.'

Tom put her bags into the vehicle and took out a set of body armour. As he handed it to her he said, 'You know how to get into this?'

'Sure, Tom, thanks.' She checked the Kevlar plates were insitu, adjusted the shoulder straps and deftly slipped the heavy protection over her head. After securing the vest with Velcro side straps, she shrugged her shoulders and moved the armour into a comfortable position on her torso. 'Okay, I'm good,' she said to no one in particular.

'Looks like you've done that once or twice before,' said Danny, with mild admiration.

'More than once or twice, honey,' she said, as she winked.

'Right. Let's move.' said Jack, 'Lisa, you're in with me and Tom.

'Spoilsport,' joked Danny.

* * *

Thirty uneventful minutes later, the two vehicles passed through the gates of Castle's compound. They drove over to the covered parking area and dismounted the vehicles, thankful of the shade in the forty degree sunshine.

'Santosh, will you sort, Lisa out with a cabin please?' said Jack.

'Okay, boss,' replied Santosh, as he collected her bags from the Landcruiser.

'Get settled in, Lisa, you'll want a shower, too. Soon as you're ready we'll see you over at my place.'

'Okay, Jack, see you later.'

Jack and Tom watched her walk away as Tom said, 'What's the plan?'

'I'd like to get her on the next flight out, but I have a feeling that's not going to happen,' replied Jack, as he shook his head.

'I think you're right, mate,' grinned Tom.

'Okay, let's get a drink at my place and wait for Ms Reynard,' said Jack.

Tom sat on the small couch drinking from a can of Red Bull. As he looked around the room he smiled to himself at the way his friend had made the place efficient and comfortable. All the cabins were the same size and had the same facilities, the most important being the excellent air-conditioning system. Jack had hung some nice pictures of the Lake District and a couple of healthy looking house plants made the place quite civilized, until you looked at the wall rack, which held his body armour and weapons.

'So what else do you know about, her?' said Tom, 'I know about her being here in 2003, with the marines, but that's pretty much it. What else has she done?'

'I talked to her quite a bit when we were in the hotel, back in 2003. She's a very capable woman, buddy. She's been with the Washington Post since she left college. Her first conflict zone was Mogadishu, at the height of the civil war. She was just a junior, probably twenty three, or four, but apparently she did some brilliant work and got noticed.

'That was a bad place to be, in the 90s,' said Tom, 'Blackhawk Down and all that shit.'

Jack grinned and nodded at the movie reference, then continued. 'After that, she spent a year in central Africa, Chad, Congo, Cameroon.'

'Oh, nice, all the high spots,' said Tom.

'Then, she was with the Brits in Afghanistan, I think she was there for about a year, based out of Camp

Bastion. When the shit hit the fan here in 2003 she moved to the Post's local bureau in Baghdad. She was embedded with the marines for about six months; saw a lot of action with the yanks on patrol, she was out day and night with them. I read something about her being in South America recently, working the drug cartels, in Colombia.'

'Well, I guess she should be okay with our bunch then.'

'She's a great looking woman, no doubt about that, but she's a smart lady. And tough!'

The conversation ended with a rhythmical knock on the door and without waiting to be asked, Lisa came in, 'Hi, guys,' she said with a beaming smile.

'Hi. Have a seat. We were just talking about you.'

'Really? And what might you be talking about?'

'Oh, I was just telling, Tom what a rubbish journalist you were.'

'Right,' she said smiling, 'Best he knows that from the start, eh, honey?'

Jack took a couple of bottles of water from the fridge, 'You want one of these, Tom?'

'Yeah, cheers.'

He handed the other to Lisa, who looked around the room and said, 'This is very civilised, gentlemen.'

They each took a mouthful of water, then Jack said, 'Excuse my French, but what the hell are you doing here, Lisa?'

'Aw, don't be like that honey, I'm here to help.'

'You could help via Skype, if there was anything we needed to ask,' said Tom.

'Yes, but that's no fun sweetie, so I'm going for the stones with you.'

Tom looked at Jack and shook his head, 'I told you, mate.'

'Look, I'm a respected journalist and experienced war correspondent. I haven't just rocked up here on a whim. I'm here first, in a professional capacity and second, coz you are a friend Jack and I believe I can help find the stones. I'm not stupid and I'm certainly not some feeble female.'

'I know all that,' said Jack, 'But it'll be uncomfortable at best and most certainly dangerous.'

'I get it, honey, but you shouldn't concern yourself about my safety, it's my decision.'

'Everyone's safety is my concern,' he said indignantly. 'That's my job and whether you go with us, is not your decision. It's ours.'

'You know my background, you know what I've done over the last ten years,' she said defensively.

'Yes I do, but you won't be with the marines this time,'

'Look, I can help. I really can. Especially when we find the diamonds. I have some great contacts in the Middle East. We may need, when we come to return them to the Kuwaitis.'

'I'm sure you'd be an asset at that time, so why not get a flight down to Dubai and wait there 'till we find the stones?' said Jack.

'Like I said, honey. No fun.'

'Okay, I'm not going to argue, Lisa, your choice.'

'Are you serious?' said Tom, 'God knows what we're gonna run into. We're using the old smugglers' route along the Tigris, and that's all bandit country.'

'Let's wait and see how things pan out once we talk to the guys. We'll make a final decision then.'

'Can you use a weapon?' said Tom.

'Tom, I may sound Manhattan, but I was born on Long Island. I'm fourth generation mafia and I can use a side arm as well as you can, sweetie.'

'Okay,' said Jack, 'You understand this mission is off-the-grid, so there'll be no insurance cover, *if,* we decide to take you along.'

'Who needs insurance,' she said, as she raised her hands. 'We're off to dig up twenny kilos of diamonds.'

Chapter Twelve
'The Plan'

The sign on the Recreation Hall door said, BRIEFING IN PROGRESS. Inside, Ali Wassam, now without crutches, sat next to Santosh on one of the small couches, watching American football on TV. Ian, Danny and Steve stood by the drinks machine getting coffees when Tom, Jack and Lisa arrived. Santosh immediately switched off the TV and stood up.

'You want coffee, Lisa,' said Danny.

'Just water, please.'

'I'll have a coffee, please, Daniel,' said Tom, in an effeminate voice.

'Piss off, you can get your own.'

'Okay, guys, let's get to it.' said Jack.

Everyone took a seat and the room fell silent, as Jack Castle began the story of Colonel Omar and the Kuwaiti diamonds.

Twenty minutes later the room was still in silence. 'Is this true?' said Ian.

'Every word,' said Lisa

Ian turned to Jack. 'So the old boy who died here a few days ago: he really was the guy who found the Kuwaiti Landcruiser, he was'nae just Tonto?'

'What old boy?' said Lisa, 'And what's Tonto?'

'Tonto means you're crazy,' said Danny.

'We had an old Iraqi here the other day. He freaked out when he saw the Kuwaiti Landcruiser, said Tom 'He told us how he'd found it on the roadside and brought it to Baghdad.'

'Can we talk to him?' said Lisa excitedly.

'As I just said,' added Ian, 'the old boy died.'

'But it does give more credence to the story, even though hugely coincidental,' said Jack.

'So we know the story is Kosher and we have a map with the location of a shit load of diamonds,' said Steve. He removed the eye patch and rubbed the socket, 'When do we leave?'

'Firstly everyone needs to understand this will be an 'off the grid' mission,' said Jack.

'Anyone who doesn't want to go, say so now,' said Tom, 'How about you Ali?'

'Fack it, I'm in, boss,'

'Me too,' said Santosh, as he flashed his big smile.

'Okay,' said Jack, 'this is the plan,'

At the end of the briefing, Jack said, 'Any questions?'

'Sounds good to me,' said Steve.

'Yeah, cool,' added Danny.

'Santosh and Ali nodded agreement.

'Ian?' said Tom,

'Aye, I'm good, just thinking what I need to take.'

'Yeah, right, let's go through responsibilities now,' said Jack.

Lisa stood up and said, 'Err excuse me, but I don't understand why we need to make such a big detour to go south, why not just go straight down Highway One, we'd be there in a day.'

'That's true' said Jack, 'But H-one is crawling with US convoys and checkpoints. We need to stay low profile.'

'And what is this Knights Templar route you're talking about?' she continued.

'The Knights Templar,' said Jack, 'Were crusaders,'

'Yes I know who they were,' she replied with feigned indignation. 'But what about this route?'

'The knights travelled from the Holy Land, down through Kurdistan and along the River Tigris, to the port at Umm Qasr. From there they took ships to southern India and traded with the Moguls. They offered their services as mercenaries and were paid in vast sums of silver,'

'Right. Okay,' she said, 'then it's fitting we travel the knights' route to find our treasure.'

'Rock and roll,' said Danny.

The hall suddenly seemed to fill with an air of excitement and everyone was talking at once.

'Calm down please, let's get responsibilities defined,' said Tom.

Jack continued with the briefing, 'Right, three vehicles. Me, Tom and Lisa in Vic 1, Steve and Danny in Vic 2, Ian, Santosh, Ali, Vic 3, okay? Arms and ammo. Steve, Danny, get everyone's weapons and give them a full service. Fill out your ammunition request and anything else you need and Tom will sign it off.'

'Okay, boss,' said Steve.

'Ian, check the medical kits in the vehicles and bulk up the equipment for possible triage.'

'Nae bother. I'll take plenty of saline and a de-fib unit, just hope we'll nae need it.'

'Santosh, Ali, plenty of fuel and water and extra spare wheels, sort out some food as well.'

'Yes, boss,' said Santosh, 'What about tents?'

'No need, we'll sleep in the Landcruisers. Ian, you'll cover comms as well. Check the shortwave radios in the vehicles and put a satellite phone in each one. Tom will sign out a satellite scanner for you. Once we're in the desert we'll need to know who's out there.'

'Okay, you all know what to do,' said Tom. 'Get everything ready and we'll meet for dinner at 18:00. Might as well get a decent meal tonight, it'll be our last for a few days. Ali, you better get home, let your wife know you'll be away for a while.'

'And, Ali, not a word to anyone about this mission eh?' added. Jack.

* * *

Ali Wassam drove out of the Green Zone and continued down the road for about two hundred metres. He parked in a small tree-shaded layby, got out and opened the boot. He struggled to pull out the old cloth bundle concealed in the underside of the boot lid. He took the bundle back into the car and unwrapped it, revealing a shiny leather pouch. He unfastened the pouch and took out a brand new satellite phone, switched it on and pressed one key. He waited for a few seconds, the phone against his ear; then a shiver went down his spine, as a quiet voice said, 'Salaam, brother.'

Chapter Thirteen
'Morning Coffee Anyone'

The half-light of the early morning, had the birds in the Green Zone chirping already. The sun had not yet risen and the sky to the west was still dark. It would not be daylight for another half hour, but the three Landcruisers were already loaded and ready to go. The team was assembled, with full body armour and weapons. Spirits were clearly high as they joked and sipped hot coffee. Jack Castle and Tom Hillman arrived and Jack said, 'Morning, guys, everyone good?'

'Morning, boss, all ready to go,' replied Ian.

'What no, Lisa?' said Tom.

'Maybe we can get away without her,' joked Jack.

'I heard that, Mr Castle.'

'Okay. Now we're all here, let's mount-up,' said Tom.

They boarded their respective vehicles, Jack was taking the first stint as driver, with Tom next to him and Lisa in the back.

Danny climbed into the driver's seat in Vic 2, Steve rode shotgun. Ali was in his usual rear gun position in Vic 3, with Santosh driving and Ian up front with the satellite scanner.

The engines started up, the lights were switched on and Jack's voice was heard through the individual earpieces, 'Good to go?'

'Good to go,' from Santosh.

'Good to go,' from Danny.

Jack turned to Lisa and said, 'You okay, you ready for this?'

'Oh yes, sir,' she replied, with a nod of her head.

Jack spoke into the throat mic again, 'Okay, ladies, let's rock and roll.'

'Rock and roll,' shouted Danny. 'Let's go get rich.'

Ian switched on the dashboard CD and flipped it to loudspeaker. As they moved away from the parking area the rest of the compound was rudely awakened by Marilyn Monroe singing 'Diamonds are a girl's best friend'.

Miss Monroe was silenced as they exited the gates and the team's mood immediately switched from jocular to 'business as usual alert'. They would be in harm's way and each individual knew, once out of the city, they would be on their own. Castle's plan was good and each one would contribute to the mission in their own way, but they would need to be a cohesive unit that thought and responded as one, if they were going to find the treasure and get back safely.

They did not take the usual route out of the Green Zone, but instead drove east towards the Tigris River and The

14th of July Bridge, exit. They crossed the bridge slowly, then stopped and waited to be called forward by the sentry. The guard waved and they eased the small convoy forward, each vehicle stopped in turn to show ID's and then passed through the checkpoint. They exited the secure area and within a few seconds were driving through the streets of the Karadah District.

The convoy drove as fast as was possible along the crowded roads. Castle expertly manoeuvred the big Landcruiser in and out of the local cars and lorries. The two vehicles behind kept pace with the lead, all driving in close formation, so as not to allow any other vehicle to split them up. These streets were just as dangerous as anywhere else in the city and the only real protection was the ability to move at speed and never stop.

They headed through the busy commercial area of Karadah, with its shops and street side cafes. The pavements were as busy as the roads, even at this early hour, with people going to work, groups of children laughing on their way to school and women, some in western clothes, others in traditional burkas, buying from street stalls piled high with fruit and vegetables. This view of the city gave the impression of hope and prosperity, but in reality Baghdad and Iraq, was a city and nation in turmoil, infected by tribal, political and religious division, governed by a foreign power and suffering from underinvestment and non-regeneration. The resentment by most of the population towards the governing and occupying powers was evident and the number of attacks on coalition bases and assets had steadily risen over the last few years. Post Saddam Iraq was getting worse, not better.

'This is a shitty area to be in,' said Tom.

'Yeah, just so busy this part of town and we are coming up on the Salah Mosque junction.'

'What's that?' said Lisa.

'Six roads go into the junction, it's always congested, pretty dangerous place to get stuck,' Jack replied.

'It's a favourite place for rooftop snipers, because security and coalition vehicles have to move so slowly through the area,' added Tom.

The junction was now a hundred metres in front of them and the heavy traffic was already slowing down, far less than was comfortable for the small convoy.

'Looks like the junction is totally jammed,' said Tom.

'I'm not going into that lot and definitely not stopping,' announced Jack.

The three Landcruisers were bumper to bumper and moving at five kliks an hour; even the pedestrians walked faster and those that didn't, slowed down to look into the vehicles.

'Keep close, guys,' said Jack into his throat mic.

The headlights were on full beam; Jack switched on the red and blue warning lights and for good measure flipped on the siren. The pedestrians alongside backed away from the vehicle as Jack gunned the engine and swung the steering wheel hard to the right; the big tyres easily mounted the kerb. He straightened up and edged forward waiting for the other two Landcruisers to mount the walkway.

'Okay, all on the pavement boss,' confirmed Santosh in the rear.

'Copy,' said Tom.

Jack increased speed and was able to make good headway through the irate, fist waving pedestrians and cheering children. They were twenty metres from the corner and would be out of the danger zone in a few seconds, but as the crowd parted in front of them Tom said, 'Oh this is gonna be fun.'

There were about a dozen people seated, eating breakfast, at a pavement side café. As soon as the crowd parted and the diners saw the big armoured cars bearing down on them, panic set in and they ran everywhere, cups, plates and food was knocked off tables and scattered across the floor. Jack kept the vehicles moving and drove into the tables and chairs knocking them out of the way, scattering furniture in all directions. A large slab of pitta bread flew up and stuck to the windscreen with an oily splat; Jack flipped on the washer wipers and cleared the redundant breakfast from the glass. He turned the corner and clattered through the rest of the cafes outside furniture, then bumped off the pavement back onto the road. His eyes darted from front view to rear mirror, checking his companions had navigated the coffee shop hazard. Lisa had stopped taking photographs and was laughing out loud, 'Oh that was fun,' she said delightedly. 'Just like the Italian Job.'

'You're only supposed to blow the bloody doors off,' joked Tom, 'Nicely done, mate.'

'Nice one, boss,' said Danny over the mic.

'Can we do it again?' added Santosh. 'That was brilliant.'

Chapter Fourteen
'The Dunes'

The convoy left the city without further incident and headed south east. They picked up the Eastern Highway, which runs parallel to the Tigris. The road was in reasonable condition and they made good headway, the desert to the right, the big river on their left.

'The Tigris River flows from the Taurus Mountains in eastern Turkey, through Syria and down the length of Iraq, almost two thousand kilometres to the Arabian Gulf,' said Jack.

'And how do you know that?' said Lisa.

'Oh, he's a fount of useless information,' joked Tom.

'Sumerian mythology has it, the river was created by the God Enki, in order to bring great riches to the inhabitants of ancient Mesopotamia,' continued Jack with a professorial air.

'Oh, now he's just showing off.'

'I'm impressed,' said Lisa with a smile. 'Let's hope Enki is on our side for this mission.'

They continued on the Eastern Highway for about forty five minutes and then turned onto the decidedly uncomfortable Al Kut Highway. Calling this thoroughfare a highway was like calling a donkey a Derby winner. The road had not been maintained for many years. Scarred with potholes, some as big as a car, made for difficult driving and if you drove too close to the edge, it would crack and crumble away like day old Danish pastry.

The hot wind that blew in from Iran picked up the sand and spread it over the surface of the road and in several places dunes had built up and blocked the route completely. Sixty kilometres south east of Baghdad, the Al Kut Highway had been lost to the desert and the dunes in this area were more than twenty metres high. Over the years, a track had developed around the barren hills of sand. Going around could take three hours, going over could take less than an hour.

Jack stopped his vehicle in the middle of the road. The other two Landcruisers pulled up behind and everyone dismounted. Danny and Steve, weapons ready, scanned the desert each side of the highway expecting nothing, but ever cautious and ready for anything.

'Okay,' said Jack. 'We all know about these dunes, although no one's been across them. The plan was to go over, not around but now seeing them in the flesh, they look pretty tricky. Thoughts, anyone?'

'It'll save us almost three hours, if we go over,' said Steve.

'But we could get stuck,' added Ian.

'What do you think, Ali?' said Tom.

'This track is made by carts and shitty local vehicles. They are not able to cross the big sand, but we have

Landcruisers,' replied Ali, proudly tapping the bonnet of the lead vehicle. 'All should be well.'

'Oaky, then, we're going across,' declared Jack.

'Yeah,' shouted Danny. 'Side-tracks are for pussies.'

'Right, let's take some air out of the tyres,' said Tom.

'Why take air out?' said Lisa.

'Less air makes the tyre spread, gives wider footprint, gives more traction on the shifting sand,' explained Santosh.

'Will it be dangerous?'

'Depends where the boss leads us. It'll be fun though,' he said with a huge grin.

After the tyres had been deflated, the spare wheels and fuel from the roof racks were secured inside. The rest of the supplies, ammunition, water, medical and food were stowed securely.

'Isn't it dangerous to have the fuel inside?' said Lisa.

'Yeah, but having it inside while we traverse the dunes, will lower the centre of gravity and may help to keep us upright.' answered Jack, 'Okay, everyone good to go?' he said into the throat mic.

'Good to go,' from Santosh.

'Rock and roll,' from Danny.

Jack put the Landcruiser into four-wheel-drive mode, engaged the lowest gear, slipped the handbrake and moved slowly forward to the base of the first dune. The big tyres bit into the soft sand, as Jack gunned the engine. The wheels gained purchase and the vehicle began the forty five degree climb, straight up the side of the sand hill. As the small convoy reached the top of the first dune the task ahead became clear, the Tigris was visible to the east, but it was not possible to see anything but dunes to the south or west.

'Okay, everyone strapped in?' said Jack into the mic. 'Let's have some fun,'

Jack moved off the crest of the dune and down the other side, gathering speed and kicking up a large amount of dust, as the big tyres cut into the soft sand. He eased on the brakes and changed gear as he approached the bottom of the dune, then gunned the engine to take on the next slope. Pressing the accelerator to the floor the revs built and the low gear worked in harmony. They pushed on through the shifting sand, the big engine roared and the vehicle ate up the slope. They reached the summit effortlessly and at the top of the dune he stopped and looked back at the other two vehicles, then said into the mic, 'Okay, Danny, your turn. Take it easy.'

'On my way.'

Jack, Tom and Lisa watched, as Danny moved down the first slope. Tom said, 'He's going too fast.'

'Not too fast,' instructed Jack into the mic.

Danny was almost at the bottom of the slope, he hit the brakes too hard and the front of the Landcruiser thumped uncomfortably into the sand.

'F'fuck sake, take it easy,' said Steve.

Danny managed to gain revs and gunned the engine, as Jack had done a few seconds earlier. They were now moving up the incline, the top only a few metres away. He came to a stop behind the lead vehicle, 'That was fun,' he said into the mic.

'Yeah,' replied Jack, 'just remember, its slow going down and fast going up.'

'Yeah. Got it boss.'

'Okay, Santosh, your turn,' continued Jack.

Santosh had watched the other vehicles closely and how each had moved down and up the sand hills. He turned to Ian and Ali, 'Okay, ready?'

'Let's go,' said Ian, with a 'thumbs up'.

'Okay,' from Ali, who, not having any seat belt, had wedged himself between the back seat and back door of the vehicle. Santosh moved off the first summit and was pulling up alongside the other vehicles a few moments later.

'You made that look easy buddy,' said Jack, into the mic, 'Maybe you should take the lead?'

'No thanks, boss. I'm happy to watch you two, so I can see where you fuck up.'

There was laughter in the three vehicles, as Jack moved off and took on the next sand hill.

They had made good progress and although moving relatively slowly had covered about two thirds of the distance, when suddenly the sand under the front wheels of Vic 1 gave way. They were on the downslope, of a twenty metre dune and had begun to increase speed, just as the tyres sank up to the wheel-arches. The front of the vehicle was going nowhere, but the back end pivoted round and continued to move down the slope.

'Hang on!' shouted Jack, as he tried to halt the slide, but the brakes served no purpose and the big Landcruiser slowly tipped onto its side, as if in a slow motion video, then slid down the dune, coming to rest with an uncomfortable thump, at the base.

'Fuck sake!' shouted Jack, then, 'You two okay?'

'Yes, cool, mate.' said Tom with a big grin.

'That was exciting, honey,' said Lisa.

'I suppose it could've been worse,' replied Jack.

Steve's voice came over the mic, 'You guys okay down there?'

Tom tried to open the door, but the weight of the armour made it almost impossible to move on his own. They could not get out of the rear door, as the equipment was blocking the back exit. Jack stood up alongside Tom and together they managed to push the heavy door open. With Jack's help, Tom climbed out and knelt on the side of the vehicle. Sweat already trickled down his face and the settling dust made him cough and splutter. Lisa had climbed over the seats; then Jack helped her up, as Tom pulled her clear of the stricken vehicle.

Vic 2, had moved down the dune, to the right of the sand hole and safely stopped alongside Jack's vehicle.

Danny and Steve jumped out and the concern on their faces faded, when they saw the three occupants were all safe.

'Stunt driving now, eh, boss?' said Danny.

Santosh was still at the top of the dune and had exited his vehicle, 'Everything okay, down there?' he shouted.

Steve looked up and said quietly into his throat mic, 'The fucking vehicle is on its side, what d'you think? Get your arse down here.'

Vic 3 pulled up alongside Vic 2 and Ian, Santosh and Ali, piled out to join the group standing by Jack's sad looking Landcruiser.

'Right, boss, what's the plan now?' said Ian.

'Let's get all the gear out first. Then we'll see if we can pull her back on her feet.' said Jack.

Tom opened the back door and climbed in, quickly unclipping the securing straps, that held the equipment in place. Ali and Santosh came over and said, 'Get out of there, boss, we'll get the gear out.'

'I'll pass it to you. You move it away from the vehicle,' replied Tom.

'Danny, move your vehicle over there and get the big tow-line out.' instructed Jack. 'Ian, move yours over there, back it up and run out the winch. Lisa, can you help the guys unload, please?'

Once all the equipment was out and clear, Santosh climbed onto the side of the vehicle and attached the winch-cable to the chassis, as Steve clipped the tow-line onto the back axle. Santosh jumped down and got into his vehicle, Danny climbed back into his. Into his throat mic, Tom said, 'Take up the tension, guys, easy now!' The metal winch-cable went taut and gleamed in the sunlight, tight as a guitar string.

'Hold it, Santosh,' said Tom. 'Keep it going, Danny. Easy now.'

The tow-line stretched and creaked, as the tension increased. 'Right, guys, together now, slowly!' continued Tom, his arms in the air, hands moving in circles, signalling to the drivers. He watched the vehicle slowly rise from the sand, as Danny gunned the engine and moved gently backwards. Santosh expertly controlled the pace of the winch and the combined effort of the two Landcruisers, pulled the third clear of the ground and slowly up onto two wheels. 'Easy now!' shouted Tom, as he backed away from the rising vehicle. The centre of gravity shifted at the optimum point and the big Landcruiser righted itself, with a loud thump and large cloud of dust.

The watching group applauded and shouted congratulations, as Tom turned and took a bow.

Chapter Fifteen
'Blackhawks'

After another twenty minutes of uncomfortable, but uneventful sand driving, the convoy came to a stop, at the base of the last dune. Jack parked at the side of the crumbling Al Kut Highway and said, 'Let's get the wheels and fuel back on the roof racks and re-inflate the tyres.'

The other two vehicles parked close against the lead Landcruiser and everyone dismounted. Danny and Steve, ready as ever, checked in all directions to ensure they were safe. Steve went back to Santosh's vehicle and spoke to Ian, 'How's the scanner looking buddy?' he said.

'All looking pretty normal since we left the city. Nae much movement out here, but there is one thing.'

'What you got?'

'Could be nothing, but see these four blips,' Ian indicated four tiny green dots with his pen.

'Yeah,' Steve removed his sunglasses and squinted at the screen.

'I picked them up coming out of Baghdad. They've been there ever since.'

'So?' said Steve.

'They're travelling in exactly the same direction as we are.'

'Right, but they could be going anywhere,' continued Steve.

'Maybe, but when we stop, they stop as well.'

'So you think they're following us?'

'Too soon to say really. They are stopped at the moment.'

'Where?'

'Where the Eastern Highway joins the Al Kut Highway.'

'That's about an hour behind us?' said Steve.

'Aye about that, a bit more maybe.'

'Okay, let's tell the boss. Jack, Tom, check this out,' shouted Steve.

'How does the scanner work?' said Santosh.

'It's a laptop device, as you can see,' said Ian. 'It incorporates SATNAV and radar and this one has about a fifty klik range. It can pick up any moving, aircraft or vehicle, within that area.'

'Okay, got it.' said Santosh.

Ian got out of the vehicle and placed the scanner on the seat, so they could all see the screen. He then told Tom and Jack what he had just told Steve.

'Okay,' said Jack. 'So we don't know for sure if they are following us, right?

'Aye that's right, but it's too soon to tell.'

'Let's see what the score is when we make camp tonight. If they're still on the scanner this evening, then we know we may have a problem,' continued Jack.

'Can you tell what kind of vehicles they are?' said Tom.

'No, nae really. The scanner picks up the trace, it does nae give a vehicle type.'

'Okay, so it's fair to say if they come over the dunes, then we know they are 4x4's. If the come around, we know they're ordinary cars.'

'Aye, that's a fair assumption. Why?'

'Just another way of knowing who we may be dealing with,' added Jack. 'If they are 4x4's, they could be security like us, but if they are local cars, then it could be trouble.'

'Correct,' said Tom.

'Monitor them 'til we make camp this evening, Ian and watch if they come over the dunes, or go round,' instructed Jack, 'Right guys, let's move.'

The convoy continued to travel south, as fast as was possible on the beaten up old road, but their speed was impeded by the amount of potholes and large cracks on the surface. In some parts they went off road and ran three abreast across the hard sandy surface of the desert; a large dust cloud in their wake. It was late afternoon when Ian's voice came over the mic. 'Scanner's showing a couple of helicopters coming in from the east, about ten kliks out.'

'Okay, everyone stay cool, slow down, let's see if they pass us by,' replied Jack.

'Copy that,' responded Santosh and Danny.

A couple of minutes later and the helicopters came into view, closing fast on their position. It was clear they were heading directly towards the moving vehicles and within seconds the helicopters were circling above the now slow moving Landcruisers. The drivers in each vehicle slotted a small plastic Union Flag in the windshield, hoping the choppers would see they were British and carry on with their patrol. An American voice came over the short wave radio,

'Three vehicles heading south, please identify.'

Tom picked up the handset and pressed the send button, 'We are a British security team, on route to Basra.'

There was silence for a several seconds, then the American voice said, 'Please stop your vehicles sir.'

'What's the problem?' said Lisa.

'We're in an area not usually travelled by coalition vehicles, they're gonna want to know what we're doing out here,' replied Tom.

'Everyone be cool,' said Jack into his throat mic. 'I have an idea. Stay in the vehicles.'

One of the choppers had landed about fifty metres in front of the convoy and was kicking up a dust cloud, the other was hovering fifty or sixty metres away to the right. The side door gunner had his 50 calibre machine gun trained menacingly on the standing vehicles.

'Let's go, Tom, you, too, Lisa.'

'What's the deal?' she said.

'Just follow my lead; you have your passport and ID?'

'Yes, they're here,' she replied, tapping the big pocket in the leg of her trousers.

All three put on sunglasses against the unpleasant dust and dismounted the Landcruiser. They walked slowly towards the Blackhawk. The door gunner had his 50 cal trained on the approaching group. His shiny black visor covering his face made him look decidedly sinister.

A marine lieutenant appeared from around the front of the chopper and waved them forward with his left hand; he held a gun in the right.

'Please keep your hands where we can see them,' shouted the officer.

'Good morning,' said Jack as they approached the lieutenant.

'Morning.' The reply was courteous, but not too friendly.

'IDs, please,' he said, 'Nice and easy.'

The two handed over their Department of Defence badges and after checking them, the officer's demeanour changed noticeably. He slipped the sidearm into his shoulder holster and said, 'What you guys doing all the way out here?'

'This is Lisa Reynard. She's with the Washington Post, doing a story about the villages along the Tigris. We're her security team. Lisa, let the Lieutenant see your passport and ID, please.'

Smiling, she fished out the documents and passed them to the officer, 'Here ya go.'

After checking her documents, he handed them back with a, 'Thank you ma'am.'

He turned to Jack. 'Okay sir, you're good t'go. Be careful in the Amarah region, there's a lot of bandits operating.'

'Thanks lieutenant, you guys have a safe day.'

They all shook hands and as the officer saluted he said, 'Same to you, sir.'

He raised his hand above his head and made a circular gesture, indicating all was good and they were ready to leave. The three moved slowly back, as the rotors gained speed and the Blackhawk rose into the clear blue sky. Jack shielded his eyes against the swirling dust and then smiled as he returned the wave from the sinister door gunner.

The three returned to the vehicles and Jack walked over to Ian. 'Anything on the scanner?'

'Our four friends are still heading this way and they went around the dunes, nae over.'

Tom joined them and said, 'What's the score?'

'The four vehicles are still heading this way,' said Jack.

'They could be just going tae Al Kut,' added Ian.

'Maybe, but you don't usually get four vehicles together, that all stop at the same time as we do?'

'We should be well past Al Kut before dark. Once we stop for the night, we can see what these muppets do. Keep a close eye on them, Ian. Well done, good job,' said Jack.

'Nice work, buddy, ' said Tom, as he slapped Ian on the shoulder.

After Tom and Jack left, Santosh said, 'If they are following us, how do they know which way we are travelling and how do they know when we have stopped?'

'They could have a scanner too.' answered Ian, 'or they're picking up a signal from us.'

'Are we sending a signal?'

'No, we're 'off the grid' so the transponders are switched off.'

'So what else would send a signal?'

'A satellite phone, but they are off as well, even if they were on, they'd have to know the phone numbers to home in on.'

'Weird,' said Santosh.

'Might nae be anything tae worry about, let's see later.'

In the back of the vehicle, Ali Wassam listened to the two men and said nothing. His current mood did not appear to be anything other than his usual surly disposition. He appeared normal, but Ali's mind was back in Baghdad with his family and his thoughts of what he had to do to protect them.

Chapter Sixteen
'Moon Over Parador'

The group of vehicles continued south, along the Al Kut Highway. The ride was uncomfortable, as the big vehicles swerved and dodged the larger potholes and bounced through the smaller ones. It was early evening and they had passed the town of Al Kut over two hours ago. In the west, a spectacular crimson and gold sunset had formed.

'Oh my God, look at that sky,' said Lisa.'

'Yeah, you get some amazing sunsets out here in the desert,' said Tom.

To the east, the Tigris had already slipped into darkness and a platinum moon hung in the sky.

'Gonna be dark soon, better look for a safe place to stop for the night,' declared Jack.

They continued on in silence for a few more kilometres, then Tom pointed to a couple of old buildings, set back off the road, about two hundred metres away. 'Over there,' he said.

'Yeah, I see it. Let's take a look,' replied Jack. Then into the mic, 'We're gonna check out the buildings to the right.'

'Copy that,' from Santosh.

'Copy,' from Danny.

The Landcruisers bounced off the road surface, onto the desert and drove cautiously towards the small clump of derelict buildings. The vehicles stopped about thirty metres from the old houses and Jack said into the mic, 'Steve, Danny, you're with me. Let's check this out.' Then turning to Tom. 'Back us up from here.'

'Will do.'

Danny, Steve and Jack, with MP5 at the ready, walked slowly towards the cluster of old buildings.

'Danny, go left, Steve, take the right.'

They each moved closer and it soon became evident, the place had been abandoned for many years.

'All okay here,' shouted Danny.

'Nothing here,' from Steve.

Jack spoke into the throat mic, 'All clear, Tom. Bring the vehicles up.'

Tom and the rest of the team drove the vehicles up to the clump of buildings and parked at the rear, out of sight of the highway. Lisa jumped out of the vehicle. She, stretched her arms out wide, then rubbed her backside.

'Need any help with that?' said Danny, a big grin on his face.

'I'm good for now, honey,' she said with a smile.

'I've told you t'calm down, tiger,' chided Steve.

'Just offering to help,' replied Danny, with a shrug.

'Okay to make a fire, get some hot drinks made?' said Santosh.

'Yeah, you'll be out of sight if you set up in the middle building, keep it small though. Okay buddy,' said Tom.

'Cheers, boss,'

Ali pulled some old wood from the window frames, while Santosh gathered dried grass. They had a small fire burning within minutes and water on the boil for hot drinks.

Steve and Danny had taken a walk around the perimeter, to satisfy themselves the location was secure. Jack, Tom and Ian were studying the scanner.

'So what's the deal with our four friends, Ian?' said Jack.

'Looks like they've travelled exactly the same route as us, except for the dunes, they went round them,' replied Ian

'So they passed Al Kut then?' said Tom.

'Yep, and the scanner is showing they have stopped as well.'

'Yes, but it's dark now. No one would travel that shitty road at night,' continued Tom.

'True,' confirmed Ian, 'But they've kept distance with us, pretty much since we left Baghdad and when we stop, so do they, that's too much of a coincidence.'

'Ian's right,' said Jack, 'so they must be using a scanner, same as we are.'

'Well, that's nae strictly true,' said Ian.

'How d'you mean?' said Tom.

'Look at the screen, there are many signals, dots that represent vehicles moving within a fifty klik radius of us.'

'Yeah, okay,' said Tom.

'We can see all these vehicles, but we'd no be able tae track a particular vehicle, unless we were homed in on a transponder signal from them.'

'So you're saying these four vehicles, that have been supposedly following us since Baghdad, are homed in on a signal from us?' said Jack.

Ian looked at the screen for a few moments and said, 'Aye, I think they could be.'

'So where's the fucking signal coming from?' said Tom. 'Our location transponders are switched off and so are the satellite phones, or they should be. I'll go and check them.'

A few minutes later Tom returned with the three satellite phones.

'All these are off and they'd need the numbers to track them anyway.'

'Lisa,' shouted Jack, 'Can we have a word please?'

'Hi, what's up?'

'Have you got a satellite phone?'

'Yeah, I'd never go on an assignment without one, is there a problem?'

'No,' said Jack, 'but could you bring it over please?'

Lisa returned and handed the phone to Jack, who passed it to Ian, 'This is off,' he said.

'Yes, of course. I only switch it on if I need it,' she said.

'Okay, Lisa,' said Jack, as he took the phone from Ian and handed it back. 'Please don't switch it on.'

'Look,' said Ian. 'We're heading towards Amarah, they could be going there. Maybe we're a wee bit paranoid.'

'Maybe,' said Jack, 'But we watch these fuckers like a hawk and post guards tonight.'

'Agreed,' said Tom, 'Now let's get something to eat, I'm starved.'

Santosh had boiled water and made coffee. He had opened a case of dried combat rations and everyone helped themselves to various packets of their choice, beef stew, chicken curry, pasta and cheese. The 'C' rations, as they were usually called, were dehydrated soya or pasta, with various flavourings, that when reconstituted produced a nourishing, if not particularly appetizing meal. He had also brought fresh fruit and energy bars, which everyone homed in on.

The group sat around the small fire and ate with relish, not because the food was tasty, but more to the fact they had not eaten for about sixteen hours. Once everyone had finished and had a hot drink, Jack stood up.

'We'll post a watch tonight, guys.'

He looked at his Rolex, it was just after nine o clock.

'I take ten till midnight, Tom and Ian, midnight till two; Danny, Steve, two till four; Santosh, Ali, four till six.'

'I can help,' said Lisa.

'Thanks, but it's okay. You get some sleep,' replied Jack.

'Let's top up the fuel before we settle down, guys,' said Tom.

Jack went back to his vehicle and took a can of Red Bull, put it in his pocket for later during his watch. Lisa stood and followed him back to the vehicle, 'I'll stand watch with you if you like?'

'No, I'm fine, Lisa. You get some sleep.'

'Okay, honey, see you in the morning.'

'Night, Lisa.'

Jack walked around the small clump of derelict buildings and back to the vehicles. The guys were settling down inside the Landcruisers, some across the back seats others reclining in the front. Jack stopped at his vehicle and said to Tom, 'You okay, buddy? We did well today.'

'I'm good, Jack. Yeah we did fine. How you feeling?'

'My back's aching a bit, but I'm cool, see you in a couple hours.'

He looked over the back seat, 'You okay there, Lisa?'

'I'm fine, honey, thanks.'

'Okay, night.'

Danny and Steve had settled down in their vehicle. Santosh and Ali were stretched out in the reclined front seats; Ian was in the back, the scanner still open, the green glow of the screen illuminated his face. Jack opened the back door, 'How's it looking ?'

'Our friends are still parked up, I dinnae think we've much tae worry about tonight.'

'Let's hope not,' said Jack. 'Get some sleep buddy.'

Jack moved away from the vehicles and found a place where he could watch the road in both directions. The moon was almost full and he could see a wide area of desert to the west and north. The moon's light created shadowy Orc-like shapes across the desert floor.

He settled down with his back against a low broken wall and opened the Red Bull. He tilted his head back to drink and was overwhelmed by a sense of insignificance, as he looked at the spectacular star-studded, velvet sky. 'Wow,' he said in a low voice.

'Wow, what?' said Lisa, as she approached from the shadows.

'Just appreciating one of nature's great beauties,' he replied softly. 'The desert sky at night.'

She looked up and after a few seconds said, 'Yeah I see what you mean, wow indeed.'

She sat down next to him, back against the old wall and he offered her a drink from the can, she took a small sip and handed it back.

'Why aren't you sleeping?' he said. 'It's been a long day for you and God knows what tomorrow will bring.'

'I'll sleep later and I'm a lot tougher than I look, Mr Castle, so don't worry about long days.'

She smiled and continued, 'Just thought I'd stand watch with you.'

'Yeah, I guessed you might, that's why I didn't argue earlier,' he replied, 'Nice to have some company. Although I was enjoying the moon.'

'Yes, it's pretty spectacular out here,' she agreed.

'Moon Over Parador,' said Jack.

'That's right. A great film.' She smiled again.

She leaned closer and he could smell the faint aroma of soap on her skin. She looked into his eyes and touched his cheek, then gently kissed his lips. When he did not return the kiss, she leaned back and said, 'I'm sorry, Jack, I just had to do that.'

'It's okay, Lisa. You are an amazing woman, but...'

She stopped him in mid-sentence. 'But, you love, Nicole.'

'Yes, but, I don't just love her, I'm in-love with her.'

'Hmm, then, she is a very lucky lady.'

'No, I'm the lucky one. Ever since I met her, I've been the lucky one.'

'So, tell me. How'd you two meet?'

Jack took another drink of the warm, Red Bull, then offered the can to Lisa. She took a mouthful this time and said, 'Okay, Mr Castle, what's the story?'

Jack took another sip of the warm drink, leaned back against the old brick wall and started, 'After I left the military I was in a pretty bad way.'

'How do you mean?'

'That's another story. But for now, let's just say I was not the man I am now.'

'Right, go on.'

'I left the military and joined up with a private security company. My first gig was in Moscow, for a Russian industrialist.'

'Nicole's father?'

'Yeah, the job was to provide close protection for his daughter, while she was doing a shoot.'

'She was a fashion model?'

'Yes. She was very successful in Russia and ultimately, worldwide. She was beautiful, sorry, is beautiful.'

Lisa smiled at Jack's self-correction.

'Her mother was English and had been a beautiful woman as well.'

'Had been?'

'Yes. She died when Nicole was quite young. Anyway, Dimitri, her father, had pissed off a not-to-respectable Chechen competitor and was concerned for her safety. Nicole had been adamant she did not need protection, but her father knew the Chechen was a ruthless bastard. He had talked her into having a microchip inserted into her inner thigh.'

'That was quite radical back then, but I guess if she was a high K an' R risk ?'

'Yes. I don't think Nicole thought of it that way, but her father certainly considered kidnap and ransom, as a tactic from the Chechen.'

'Okay sorry, go on.'

'Anyway, she was staying at the Metropole Hotel.'

'That's a beautiful place, near Red Square, across the road from the Bolshoi,' said Lisa.

'That's right.'

'I met her in her suite. She was elegant, intelligent and pretty grounded, for a twenty year old woman.'

'How old were you, Jack?'

'I was thirty four, no, thirty five.'

'She was a real knockout. Any other time, I would've hit on her.'

'Oh, I'm sure you would, Mr Castle.'

'But she was my responsibility and client. That was the only way I could think of her. I stayed in the second bedroom in her suite and was with her day and night.'

'And you were never tempted?'

'Oh, I was tempted all the time,' he said with a wink and a smile.

'Go on, honey.'

'The shoot was to take ten days, around, Red Square, the Kremlin and some night work on the Moskva River.'

'All the high spots, huh?'

'Pretty much, yeah. Wasn't much to worry about during the day really. apart from getting hit on by a couple of the other models.'

'Always the lady's man.' said Lisa

'Apparently not. They said the gay hairdresser had a raging crush on me too.'

She chuckled and he offered her the Red Bull again, but she shook her head. He finished off the drink and pushed the empty can into the sand.

'We'd been there a few days and it got a little tricky. I guess she liked me and she sort of let me know it, especially in the evenings, over dinner. A couple more days passed and she made it clear she was interested.'

'And how did she do that?'

'We were in the suite. I was reading in the sitting room and she came out in this great silk robe. She looked terrific. She just came out and asked me why I had not made any advances to her.'

'What did you say?'

'I didn't have a chance to say anything. She tried to kiss me, but I put her off, as gently as I could.'

'So, was that it?'

'No, no, far from it. The next day, she was pretty cool with me. After the shoot, she said she was going for dinner with the photographer.'

'Oh how fickle, the female heart,' said Lisa, with a slight smile.

'She didn't want me to tag along, but there was no way I was letting her out of my sight. So I played gooseberry and watched the two of them eat and flirt, from a separate table.

'What was the photographer like?'

'Italian, pretty good looking, very cool.'

'Mmm yummy.'

'Yeah right.'

'So, what happened?'

'He came back to the suite and they had a few more drinks. Nicole was a bit worse for wear. It was the last night of the shoot, so I guess she wasn't bothered about getting smashed. I suggested the photographer should leave, but she said it was none of my business and took him into her room.'

'What did you do?'

'Not much I could do really. I heard the door lock and Nicole laughing. So I settled down in the sitting room.'

'You never went to bed?'

'No, not while she was alone with the Italian.'

'So, did he stay all night?'

Jack smiled and said, 'Err, no, he didn't.'

'Okay?'

'After a while, I heard her shout. I went to the door and asked if everything was ok. The door was locked, but I knocked and asked again. The Italian told me to fuck off and I heard Nicole shout, no, again.'

'So?'

'So I kicked the door in.'

'Subtle.'

'Yeah, I thought so. The Italian was naked and standing over her. He was trying to get her to snort some cocaine. He had this little mirror in his hand.'

'What did you do?'

'She was naked except for her panties.' Jack paused.

'Having a flashback there, Mr Castle?'

'Yeah. Great boobs!'

'Go on.'

'Anyway, I knocked the mirror out of his hand and he turned to try and hit me. He was a big guy, but drunk and a civilian. I just jabbed him in the throat and he fell, gasping for breath. I dragged him out of the bedroom, through the suite and kicked him into the corridor.'

'He was still naked?' she said, with a chuckle.

'Yes. When I turned round, Nicole was standing there laughing. She was still only wearing panties: then the alcohol hit and she began to fall. I grabbed her, picked her up and carried her back into her room. I put her to bed, pulled a chair up alongside the bed and settled down for the night, to keep an eye on her.'

'You stayed by her side, all night?'

'Yeah. I fell asleep in the chair. It was daylight when I felt her hand on my face. She was in her robe and sat down on my knee.'

'And?'

'She kissed me. I can remember the taste of toothpaste, on her lips. She kept on kissing me and put her arms round me.'

'What did you do?'

'I kissed her right back. And have been with her, ever since.'

Chapter Seventeen
'Nice Rolex'

Sunrise warmed the cool air of the departing night. Everyone had managed to get some sleep. Santosh had made a fire and fresh hot coffee gave off a homely aroma, around the clump of derelict buildings. Spirits were high and the thought of finding the diamonds later in the day, was a cause for joviality. After a breakfast of fresh fruit and energy bars, Jack and Tom went over to Ian's vehicle. 'How's it looking?' said Jack.

Ian, hunched over the scanner, never answered for a few seconds and then said, 'Sorry, just had tae save some data. Our pals are still in the same place as last night.'

'Okay,' said Jack. 'Let's see what happens when we pass Amarah. If they're still on our tail, then we decide on a strategy.'

'I'd still like to know how they're homing in on us, if there's no signal,' said Tom.

'Okay, guys, let's get moving,' shouted Jack.

The usual radio checks were completed and the big Landcruisers moved away from their night's shelter and back onto the beaten up old highway. The river could be seen clearly, as it shimmered in the morning sun, winding its way south to the Arabian Gulf. Those

Templars must have had a hell of a journey, Jack thought to himself.

The road had improved to some extent and the small convoy was able to move a lot faster than the previous day. The sun was high in the sky now and the heat haze caused a flickering mirage on the desert ahead. Jack eased off the accelerator, as soon as he saw the roadblock in the distance. 'Who the hell is that,' he said.

'No idea,' replied Tom, 'but out here it's definitely not the Americans.'

'Maybe we should get off the road and go around them,' suggested Lisa.

'No, it's too late, they've seen us,' said Tom, 'And the desert is mined.'

'How do you know that?' she said.

'See those burnt out vehicles each side of the road?' continued Jack.

'Yeah, so?' she said, and then realising said, 'Ah, ok, mines, right.'

'Yep, mines.'

The convoy slowly approached the makeshift checkpoint, as Steve's voice came over the radio.

'What's the deal boss?'

'Could be tribal militia, but probably bandits,' replied Tom.

'Okay guys, soon as I stop, assume defensive posture.' ordered Jack.

'Copy that,' from Danny.

'Okay boss,' from Santosh.

Jack stopped his Landcruiser in the middle of the road. Danny drove his vehicle to the left and parked at an angle. Santosh moved his vehicle to the right and stopped in a similar manner. To the uninitiated, it looked like the drivers had parked haphazardly, but in reality they had created a defendable configuration.

'Tom, you're with me. Lisa, stay in the vehicle and get down.'

Into the throat mic he said, 'Ali, I need you with us.'

'Okay, boss.'

The rest of the team swiftly exited their vehicles and took position behind the heavily armoured doors, weapons ready. Ali joined Tom and Jack and the three waited for instruction from the roadblock. A scruffily dressed individual appeared from the sand encrusted tent, at the road side. He appeared to command some respect from the other scruffy individuals, so Jack assumed he was the leader. The leader put on sunglasses, unslung the AK47 from his shoulder and gestured for them to come forward, 'No guns,' he shouted in English.

Jack, Ali and Tom, their hands raised slightly, moved in silence towards him.

Steve quickly assessed the opposition and spoke softly into his throat mic, 'Four on the barricade, plus the idiot out front, God knows how many in the tent.'

'There's nae one in the tent, said Ian softly. 'Three Landcruisers showing up would bring everyone out, there's only five o' these muppets.'

'You're probably right,' said Steve.

Ali extended his hand and said, 'Salaam Alikum.'

'Alikum Salaam,' replied the leader, without taking the offered hand.

'What are you doing here? You are not permitted to travel this road,' said the leader, a definite air of menace in his voice.

'We are heading to Basra,' replied Ali with a smile.

'You cannot pass this way; you must also pay a tax for being here.'

'What's he saying, Ali?' said Jack.

Ali moved closer to Jack and spoke quietly 'He said we can't pass and he wants money.'

'Ask him how much he wants to let us pass,' said Jack.

Ali did as he was told and the leader became irritated. 'I said you cannot pass, but you will still pay the tax.'

'Sidi, we need to travel this road. We must meet another of our friends in Amarah,' pleaded Ali, 'How much tax to let us pass?'

The leader looked at the foreigners and said, 'Okay, it will be ten thousand American.'

Ali grinned and turned to Jack and Tom, 'This facking idiot wants ten grand.'

'Fuck him,' said Tom.'

'Yes, indeed,' replied Jack, 'Tom, go back to the vehicle and bring a grand.'

Tom raised his hands and nodded to the leader, moved slowly backwards, then turned and went to his vehicle.

He opened the glove box and counted one thousand dollars, from a thick wad of cash.

From her prone position on the back seat, Lisa said, 'What's happening, Tom?' She had her camera out and was obviously keen on getting some shots. Tom saw the camera and said, 'Shit's gonna happen, stay down and don't try to photograph these idiots.'

He picked up his Glock, quietly cocked the weapon and slotted a round into the chamber. He flipped the safety catch to off and very carefully slipped the gun into the back of his belt. Returning to the barricade, he handed the cash to the Jack.

'Tell him we do not carry that much money,' said Jack, 'This is all we can spare.' He handed the dollars to the leader, who expertly flicked through the bundle, counting each note. The man said something to Ali and Ali translated, 'He says you have a nice Rolex.'

Jack unclipped the watch and handed it over. The leader smiled, rattled the watch next to his ear, stuffed it in his pocket and said in English, 'Okay, you go now.'

Tom's arm was behind his back, the sidearm in his hand. He eased the gun out of his belt and held it at his side, as he turned away from the barricade. Jack and Ali turned and had only taken a couple of steps, when they heard the metallic click of the leader's AK 47 being cocked.

Ali and Jack fell to the ground simultaneously. In a single motion Tom spun, dropped to his knee and shot the leader in the forehead, then hit the ground as Steve, Danny, Ian and Santosh took out the four muppets at the barricade. The whole incident lasted about three seconds; the muppets never fired a shot. Jack stood up and brushed off the dust. 'Cheers buddy,' he said to Tom. The rest of the guys had joined them at the barricade and Ian checked the bodies to make sure they were all dead. Danny and Steve had taken positions each side of the road, weapons ready for any trouble that may arrive, while Santosh cleared the makeshift roadblock.

'You okay, Ali?' said Jack,

'Okay, boss,' he replied with a rare grin. Then turning to Tom, said, 'Thanks, boss.'

Tom gave him a thumbs-up and winked.

Lisa had come to the barricade, camera in hand. 'I told you to stay in the vehicle,' said Jack, 'Get back there now.' He turned her round and pushed her towards the Landcruisers. She resisted and said, 'So who were these guys and why did you have to kill them?'

'Bandits and if we hadn't killed them, we'd be lying there now,' replied Tom, annoyed at being questioned.

'Get back in the vehicle please, Lisa,' said Jack again, 'Ali?'

'Yes, boss?'

'Put the bodies in the tent.'

'Okay, boss.'

'And, Ali.'

'Yes, boss?'

'Get the grand and my Rolex, please.'

Chapter Eighteen
'Roadside Delivery'

The group mounted up in silence, the joviality of the early morning gone. Each man knew what they had just done was necessary, but that did not make it any more palatable.

'Good to go?' said Jack into the mic.

'Good to go, boss,' from Santosh.

'Good to go,' from Danny.

The vehicles moved slowly through the remains of the barricade. Lisa looked at the dirty sand covered tent as they passed. Tom noticed and said gently, 'It had to be done. They had no intention of letting us get away with Landcruisers, weapons and money.'

'I know,' she said and put on her sunglasses, to hide the tears in her eyes.

The small convoy passed the junction to Amarah and continued south, the big river always on their left, the wide expanse of arid desert on the right. The highway was in reasonable condition now and occasionally they passed the odd local vehicle on the road; most likely Amarah residents travelling up and down from Basra City. In the distance a small car parked just off the road came into view and next to it stood a man waving frantically.

'Parked vic on the roadside,' said Tom into the mic, 'Standby.'

'Roger,' from Danny.

'Copy that,' from Santosh.

Jack pressed the accelerator hard down and moved to the other side of the road towards a couple of oncoming trucks. The man in the road ran across and fell to his knees, his arms in the air in a supplicatory gesture.

'There's something wrong,' said Lisa, 'Maybe we should stop.'

'No way,' said Tom, 'It could be a car bomb, suicide bomb, ambush, anything.'

Just then she saw a small boy, about five years old, get out of the parked car, 'Look,' she shouted.

'What?' said Tom annoyed.

She pointed to the boy and shouted again, 'A child, it's not an ambush.'

The convoy was moving fast now, the two trucks in front had swerved off the road, their horns blared and fists were waved from the drivers' windows.

'Stop for God's sake.'

Jack hit the brakes and brought the vehicle back across to their side of the carriageway; the man on his knees bowed his head to the ground in thanks. The child ran across to him, as the big vehicles slowed to a stop.

'Ali, go see what's the problem,' said Jack into his throat mic.

Danny and Steve were out of their vehicle, their weapons cocked ready.

'We got your back,' said Steve, as Ali walked past.

Ali walked slowly towards the parked vehicle. When he was about ten metres away, he stopped, raised his weapon and shouted something to the man. The man answered and waved for Ali to come forward. Ali moved up to the car and looked inside. His voice came over the mic.

'It's a woman, she's having a baby.'

The Landcruisers pulled off the road and parked alongside the rusty old car. Ian was inside the cramped space and Lisa was helping him. The husband stood outside and had not stopped thanking the team of foreigners who had stopped, when all others had passed him by.

'How's it going in there?' said Jack.

'Good job we stopped,' replied Ian. 'She'd never had managed to deliver on her own.'

The woman screamed again. 'Ali, come here,' shouted Ian.

'Yes boss?' he said as he stuck his head in the driver's window; then suddenly pulled back, at the sight of the woman in final stages of childbirth.

'Fuck sake, Ali, you're supposed to be a hard ass Republican Guard. Get your bloody head in there and translate,' said Tom.

'Tell her to pant quickly,'

'What you mean boss?'

'Pant,' said Lisa. 'Like this,' taking short breaths she demonstrated the instruction.

'Ah yeah,' he said.

The woman panted as Ali had instructed.

'Tell her to push hard now and keep pushing, till I say stop.'

She screamed as Ian said, 'Okay, tell her tae rest, the head is out.'

Lisa wiped the woman's face with a clean wet cloth and cradled her head.

'Okay Ali, tell her one more big push and it's done.'

Another scream and a few seconds later the faint sound of the baby's first cries.

The husband shouted, 'Allah o Akbah.'

Lisa moved out of the car and let the man in, to see his new born baby girl.

'Well done,' said Jack.

'Yes, well done indeed,' said Tom.

Ian had cleaned the mother up and made her as comfortable as possible in the back of the old car. He hooked up an intravenous line to a saline drip, which he clipped to the grab handle at the side of the car, concerned she may dehydrate, before arriving at hospital.

'Ali, tell him he needs to take her to hospital in Amarah, soon as possible.'

'He said, he was on his way there, when baby decides to arrive,' said Ali.

'Santos , give them a case of water, some fruit and energy bars,' said Jack.

'Okay, boss,'

'Check his fuel as well, if he needs some, put a can in,' added Tom, 'And give them a hundred dollars, for the hospital.'

The Iraqi shook hands with everyone in turn, then finally hugged Ian and said, 'Shukran sidi,' a huge grin on his weather beaten face. As is the custom, he did not shake hands with Lisa, but bowed several times, as he uttered blessings in Arabic.

'You have a very beautiful daughter,' said Lisa. The young boy had stood in the outside heat during the delivery of the baby. Lisa turned to him and pointed to the car, nodding for him to go and see his new baby sister. The boy ran over to her and threw his arms around her legs, holding on tight. She bent down and kissed him on his dirty forehead, his huge dark eyes sparkling in the sun. He smiled, then rushed off into the front seat of the battered old vehicle. She put her sunglasses on and, for the second time that day, had tears in her eyes.

Chapter Nineteen
'Eureka'

It was mid-afternoon and they had made good time on the Amarah-Basra highway. Traffic had increased and the three big Landcruisers attracted a lot of attention, as they sped past small roadside stalls and vehicles parked along the highway. The SATNAV indicated they were scheduled to turn off the road and head into the desert in the next thirty minutes. They would then head south west for about an hour, to the colonel's oasis.

'Ian?' Jack said into his throat mic.

'Aye, boss?'

'How's the scanner looking?'

'Our pals are still on the same route as us.'

'How far behind?'

'About an hour,' replied Ian.

'Okay. Cheers, mate.'

Then turning to Tom, Jack said, 'We turn off in the next half hour. If they carry on to Basra, then we've been paranoid. If they follow us into the desert, then we've definitely got a problem.'

'They're like a bloody itch you can't scratch,' said Tom.

In Vic 2, Danny said to Steve, 'I hope these tossers are on our tail.'

'And why would you hope that ? So we can get into a scrap?'

'Why not? Seems to me they're asking for it.'

Steve removed his eyepatch and wiped his face with a clean handkerchief; slipped the patch back in place and said, 'Daniel, we're here for a shit load of diamonds. We want to find 'em and get the fuck out of Iraq in one piece. A fight with an unknown entity, is not only stupid, it's the last thing we want, you muppet.'

'But what if we do have to take 'em on?'

'Then we do what we do best, Daniel. We make sure we're the last men standing.'

In Vic 3, Santosh concentrated on the road and maintained the fast pace set by the boss. Ian studied the scanner and made data entries into the machine, as he monitored the four green dots, which had been the focus of his attention for the last two days. In the rear gun position, Ali Wassam's mind was not on the task in hand. His thoughts were with his wife and children, as he silently prayed to God, they would be safe.

The convoy slowed and Jack's voice came over the mic, 'Okay, guys, we're going off-road.'

'Copy that,' from Danny and Santosh.

The desert was reasonably flat and compacted, punctuated by the occasional gulley, small dune and rock. They drove three abreast as the dust kicked up by the big tyres made it impossible to drive in line. The heat coming off the sand shimmered and created mirages in every direction, creating the illusion they were driving on a lake, not land. It was late afternoon and they would be at the oasis in less than an hour.

* * *

They had made good time across the hard sand and the once pristine Landcruisers were now covered in a thick layer of dust; a testament to the last forty-eight hours of hard driving.

'Is that it?' shouted Lisa, excitedly.

'Could be,' said Tom, as he checked the SATNAV.

'Yes that's it,' confirmed Jack. As he pushed down on the accelerator, an irrational thought came to him, that it may be a mirage.

'We're here, guys,' said Tom, into his throat mic.

'Magic,' from Danny.

'Copy that, boss,' from Santosh.

The vehicles slowed down, almost reverently, as they approached the colonel's oasis. The dust settled as the Landcruisers came to rest under a small clump of palm trees.

Everyone dismounted and everyone took bottles of water to quench thirsts and wash faces, much as Colonel Omar and his three accomplices had done, all those years ago. After seventeen years the 'oasis' had dried up and was overgrown, a few palm trees and bushes remained, but the small lake in the centre was now a mass of dried-out, overgrown thorn bush and scrub.

'So, this is it then?' said Danny.

'Aye, this is the location marked on the map,' confirmed Ian.

'And where do we dig?' said Lisa.

'That's the billion dollar question,' replied Tom.

'Okay, spread out, look for clues. Anything that might help us find where they may have stashed the boxes,' said Jack.

They each did as instructed and within fifteen minutes had covered the whole area with no success.

'We'd need a JCB to dig up the whole place, if we hope to find anything here,' said Tom.

'Let's think about this,' said Jack. 'We've just managed to evade an air strike and the Yanks are on our tail.'

'Yeah, go on.'

'We decide to hide the boxes. We want to do it fast, get the hell out. Right?' continued Jack.

'Yeah and this place was obviously an oasis back then, with a small lake,' said Lisa, as she spread her arms and gestured to the area in the middle of the trees.

'Correct, so where better to hide something quickly, than under water,' said Tom, 'Carry them out to the middle and let them sink.'

'That's right,' said Jack, 'We need to chop all this scrub back, see what we come up with.'

'Right, guys, get the shovels out of the vehicles and slash all these bushes down,' instructed Tom.

'Look around for some heavy branches, we can use them as well,' said Jack.

When everyone had a tool or branch, they formed a straight line at the edge of what was originally the lake.

'Nice and slow guys, make sure we cover every inch of the area.' instructed Tom.

The line moved slowly forward, slashing at the bushes and scrub, chopping it down to ground level. A few metres in, it became clear the ground sloped towards what would have been the middle of the small lake. They moved slowly forward clearing the scrub and raising a small dust cloud in the process. After several minutes and a lot of coughing, it had become difficult to see what they were doing, so Jack shouted, 'Okay, stop, everyone back.'

Back at the vehicles they all took bottles of water and drank deeply. The cloying dust had covered them from head to toe; it filled their noses, covered their hair and caked their faces.

'We'll let the dust settle, then get back in there,' said Jack.

Twenty minutes later they were back in line, chopping at the undergrowth. The ground had noticeably dropped and the bushes were now up to their chests. Profanities and expletives where abundant, as their naked arms were cut by dried branches and thorns. The line moved slowly forward; the dust was almost unbearable. They continued to cut and slash at the thick growth, right down to the old lake bed, each one secretly hoping they would be the one to find the boxes. Suddenly and with obvious delight, Danny shouted, 'Whoa! We got something.'

They coughed and spluttered in the almost blinding cloud; then moving slowly, so as not to create more dust, encircled Danny, who was now on his knees pulling away at branches and scrub. A dust covered box lay half buried in the ground, next to it a second box equally encrusted and half buried, appeared as more undergrowth was cleared. No one spoke. The atmosphere had suddenly become electric. Almost lovingly they eased the boxes from the sand's grasp, picked them up and carried them slowly back to the vehicles.

They placed the boxes on the ground and the group assembled around them in silence. Each one gulped from bottles of lukewarm water, and then splashed their 'Kabuki-like' faces, to wash off the cloying dust.

Tom knelt beside the first box and tried to unclip the securing handles on the top, but they had rusted and were immovable. He took a shovel and slashed at the handle. It broke away from the box and lid. He then did the same with the second handle. Kneeling again, he tried to remove the lid but the rubber seals had perished and had melded the lid, to the body of the box.

'F'fuck sake, are we actually gonna get the things open?' said a frustrated Danny.

Tom took the hunting knife from his belt and deftly cut around the now-solid rubber seal. A minute or so later, he put the knife between his teeth and slowly eased off the lid.

Chapter Twenty
'ISIL'

Tom lifted the lid from the dust-covered picnic box and dropped it on the sand. The box was full to the brim with small discoloured paper packets. The group watched in silence, as he took one of the packets from the treasure chest and gently opened the tiny bundle. The sun had not yet fallen below the horizon and as Tom poured the contents of the packet into his hand, its rays were caught and reflected in a thousand sparkling facets

'Yeahhhhhhh,' shouted Danny.

'Alrightie!' exclaimed Lisa.

'You fucking beauty,' from Steve.

'Och aye the noo,' said Ian, in an overtly camp, and exaggerated Highland accent.

Tom stood and looked at Jack, 'We did it, mate.' They hugged and then laughed out loud.

'Oh, you clever boys,' said Lisa, giving them both a kiss on the cheek.

Santosh stood looking into the box, a huge grin on his sweaty face, then the famous Santosh smile appeared, almost ear to ear. Only Ali Wassam, stood back and said nothing.

'Crack the other one, Tom,' instructed Jack.

Again Tom hacked off the rusty old clasps and this time part of the box broke away. He took the knife again, slit round the rubber seal and removed the second lid.

'What the fuck,' said Danny, when he saw the old Iraqi flag, stuffed into the top of the box. Tom pulled out the flag and the rotten material came apart in his hands, what lay beneath surprised them all.

'What the hell is this?' said Santosh, 'Just looks like glass rocks.'

'Uncut diamonds,' answered Tom.

'Gentlemen and lady,' said Jack, with a flourish of his arms, 'We are officially loaded.'

Santosh went to his vehicle and returned with two canvas rucksacks; then helped Danny and Tom to carefully transfer the contents of the two old boxes into the bags. When the bags were full and zipped up securely, Tom said to Santosh, 'Put them in Vic 1, mate.'

'Yes, boss,' The huge grin appeared again.

Ian had returned to his vehicle and was checking the scanner, 'Jack, Tom,' he shouted.

'What is it mate?' said Tom.

'Our friends heading this way?' said Jack.

'Aye, they're already in the desert.'

'The bastards have made up a lot of time. How long till they get here?'

'About fifteen minutes,' answered Ian.

'We have the stones, let's run for the border,' suggested Tom.

'Agreed, said Jack. 'We can easily outrun them in our vehicles.'

Lisa's scream cut through the evening air, Ali Wassam had her by the hair, a knife to her throat.

'What the fuck y'doing, Ali?' shouted Jack.

Danny and Steve, their weapons drawn had Ali in their sights.

'Yeah, what the fuck, Ali?' echoed Steve.

Lisa was at least a foot taller than the Iraqi, so she was bent over, as he pulled her head down to his level; the tip of the stiletto pressed against her skin, causing a small crimson drip to trickle down her neck. Tom and Jack had also drawn their sidearms, while Ian and Santosh looked on, with mouth open..

'So it's you that's been transmitting to these bastards?' said Tom.

'Why Ali?' said Jack. 'Haven't we treated you well?

'You'll be a rich man with your share, you could take your family anywhere.' said Tom.

'Or do you and your fucking friends want the lot?' snarled Steve, his weapon pointed straight at Ali's head. 'Say the word, Jack. I can drop this bastard in a heartbeat.'

'Cool it, Steve,' said Jack, 'Lisa you okay?'

'No, I'm not okay. There's a crazy Iraqi with a knife at my throat.'

'Ali, what's this all about?' said Jack quietly.

'They have my family, boss.' he answered, his eyes filled with tears.

'Who does?' said Tom.

'A man came to my house, he made me meet another man. He said they would kill my family if I didn't help them, he gave me the satellite phone.'

'Right and you've been sending out the signal, for these fuckers to follow us?' said Steve the gun steady in both his hands, his single eye along the sight, 'Let me just shoot this bastard.'

'Steve,' shouted Jack, 'Shut the fuck up and be cool. So who are these guys, Ali?'

'They said they were the Islamic State for Iraq,' his voice wavered and tears rolled down his weather-beaten cheeks.

'The Islamic State of Iraq and the Levant' said Jack, 'ISIL?'

'Yes, that's them.'

'Have they got your family?'

'No, but if I don't keep you here until they get the diamonds, then they will kill them.'

'Listen Ali, I can make a call now and have your family in the Green Zone in thirty minutes.'

'Make the call now,' he pleaded.

'Santosh, satphone quick.'

'Yes, boss.'

A few seconds later Santosh handed the satellite phone to Jack, who switched it on and then took out his cell phone. He found the number for Geoff Mason and punched it into the satphone.

'Geoff Mason,'

'Geoff, its Jack Castle,'

'Hi, Jack, what's up?'

'I need a seriously urgent favour. Can you help?'

'Sure, tell me?'

'One of my guys' family is at risk. I need you to bring them into the Green Zone, take them to your compound, till you hear from me. Okay?'

'What's the address?'

'Address, Ali?'

Ali called out the address and Jack relayed it to Mason.

'That's just across the river, I can have them back in the Green Zone in about twenty-five minutes.'

'Cheers, Geoff, I owe you one.'

'No problem, be safe.'

'Your family will be in the Green Zone in half an hour, Ali. Now put the knife down.'

Ali lowered the blade from Lisa's throat and let go of her hair. She rubbed her neck and looked at the blood on her fingers, then slapped him hard across the face. Steve and Danny closed in and roughly took hold of Ali, just as Ian said, 'We got company, guys.'

The sun had set and the oasis was bathed in twilight, but a dust cloud could be clearly seen in the distance and whatever was causing it, was moving towards them very fast and would be at the oasis in a few minutes.

'Too late to run now,' said Jack. 'Santosh give Ali an MP5,'

'Are you sure, boss?' said Santosh, somewhat surprised.

'Take out the magazine and make sure its unloaded first, and put the lids back on the picnic boxes.'

'Okay'

'Tom, you, me and Santosh, over here.'

'Ali, get your arse over here and hold the weapon on us.'

'Steve rig a couple of stun grenades in the picnic boxes, fast, then you and Danny into the bushes.'

'Ian, find a position on the other side of the oasis, if there's anyone left at their vehicles when the shit hits the fan, take em out.'

'Right everyone, move!'

Jack turned to Lisa and spoke quietly, 'Get in Vic 1 with the diamonds, take the keys to the other vehicles with you. If it all goes tits up, get the hell out, head in that direction and you'll hit Highway 1 in about twenty, thirty minutes. Then head south and you will be at the Safwan border crossing about an hour later, go to the military there, the rest is up to you.

'I'm not leaving you guys,'

165

'Don't argue, there's no time. Go!'

Santosh and Tom stood a few metres away from the booby trapped picnic boxes, Ali had the unloaded weapon trained on them.

Tom had his sidearm cocked and ready in the back of his belt and Santosh had concealed his MP5, in a clump of scrub at his feet.

'Good luck, guys,' said Jack.

The four vehicles rolled to a stop in a cloud of dust, their headlights illuminated the oasis.

The doors opened and a dozen men stepped out, the drivers stayed with the cars, as the other eight, all armed with AK47s walked slowly towards the group of foreigners. They were spaced out in two lines of four.

These guys are trained, definitely not bandits, thought Jack.

'Salaam Alaikum, brother,' one said to Ali. 'You have done well.'

Ali recognised him as the stranger he had met at the café and he was obviously in charge. The stranger waved to the three men at his side, instructing them to open the picnic boxes. The three moved cautiously past the foreigners, two lowered their weapons and slung them over their shoulders, as they knelt to open the boxes.

Tom, Santosh and Jack closed their eyes, just as the lids came off. The bang, flash and smoke from the stun grenade, did its job and caused the three by the boxes to fall to the ground, disorientated and temporarily blinded.

Tom dropped to his knee and in a single motion, drew the weapon, fired and shot the stranger in the forehead. Santosh fell to the ground, retrieved his MP5 and fired on the three men at the picnic boxes, killing them all. Tom and Jack now fired on the other four men rushing forward, their silhouettes illuminated in the vehicles headlights; their AK's spewing death in all directions.

Danny and Steve had already opened up on the running men, who were swiftly cut down in the cross-fire. They heard Ian shooting at the four drivers and knew he was taking return fire. Steve and Danny broke cover and sprinted towards the four cars; their weapons on full automatic, firing six hundred rounds a minute, at the remaining shooters.

After checking the four by the cars were dead, Ian, Danny and Steve re-joined the rest of the group on the other side of the oasis. The scene was carnage, twelve terrorists had been killed and miraculously none of the team had been hit, except Ali Wassam. He had been shot twice in the chest and was struggling to breathe, as the blood choked his lungs. Ian saw him and ran to help.

'Get a crash pack,' he shouted.

Lisa had already picked up the big first aid bag and handed it to Ian. After checking the wounds he said , 'I dinnae think I can do anything tae help him.'

'Boss,' croaked Ali.

'Yeah, Ali, what is it?' said Jack.

'You will make sure my family is safe, boss?'

'You have my word, Ali.'

'Thank you, I'm sorry,' then with his last breath, he whispered, 'Allah o Akbah.'

As soon as his words left his mouth, one of the four bullet riddled cars burst into flames, as if his invocation to God had been accepted. The blaze from the vehicle lit up the oasis and the stench of burning petrol permeated the still evening air.

'Santosh, get the shovels, we'll bury Ali.'

'Your joking, right?' said Steve, 'This little fucker nearly got us all killed.'

'He was trying to protect his family, Steve,' answered Tom.

Santosh had returned with the three shovels and threw two on the ground and began digging with the third; Tom and Jack picked up the others and helped him.

'Give me that, boss,' said Steve, as he took the shovel from Jack and joined the other two digging Ali's grave.

'What about the others?' said Lisa.

'They can rot,' replied Jack, 'Ian, Danny, check the Landcruisers. Make sure there's no damage.'

He stood and watched as the guys dug the grave, then bent down and went through Ali's pockets for personal effects. He removed his watch and wedding ring and took the gold chain from around his neck. He handed them to Lisa and said, 'Find something to put these in, then put them in the glove box, in our vehicle.'

She took the small pile of effects and said, 'You okay?'

He did not reply, he just stood and watched, as the grave was dug.

She looked at him and understood the respect and forgiveness he felt, for the man who had betrayed them.

Chapter Twenty One
'Safwan'

The drive across the desert to Highway One was made in silence. They hit the highway and turned south towards the Safwan border crossing. All being well, they would be there in plenty of time to beat the midnight curfew.

'What's the plan when we get to the border?' said Lisa.

'Once we cross, we'll sort out some accommodation at the military transit base,' replied Tom.

'Then what?' she continued.

'Then we shower and sleep,' said Jack.

'I've heard of the Safwan base, but never been there,' she said. 'What's it like?'

'You've been to accommodation bases in Baghdad though?' said Tom.

'Yes, several.'

'Well, Safwan's like that. It's also the main staging area for all convoys in and out of Iraq.'

'Right, so it's a busy place.'

'Yeah,very. There's hundreds of military and civilian subcontractor supply vehicles staged there, waiting to move up, or be escorted to Baghdad.'

'So we'll get accommodation ok?

'Yeah, we have contacts there, it'll be cool.'

The moon was full and high in the sky, as the three Landcruisers slowed down to join the line of vehicles waiting to cross the border. The civilian lane was about half a kilometre long and moved very slowly; there would be little chance of most of them crossing the border before the curfew.

The military lane, however, moved reasonably quickly, as anyone with the appropriate ID's or passes, were swiftly moved through.

Castle's vehicles passed through the checkpoint and exited the border facility. They drove a few hundred metres and arrived at the main entrance to Safwan Base and, after showing their ID's, were allowed entry to the huge compound. Jack took out his cell phone and pressed the number on the contacts list and after several rings a sleepy voice answered, 'Hello?'

'Charlie?'

'Yes, can I help you?'

'It's Jack Castle, buddy. Sorry t'wake you.'

'Oh. Hello, Jack, what's up?'

'We've just arrived, we need four rooms, please. Can you square it with your night manager?'

'Okay, I'll call him and tell him to expect you.'

'Thanks a lot, Charlie. Sorry again. See you in the morning.'

'It's okay. Night.'

Jack signed for the accommodation and handed out the keys. The guys would double up in twin rooms and Lisa would have a single. The rooms were pretty much the same as any other accommodation base, with basic facilities, en-suite shower and toilets, TVs, fridges, Wi-Fi, so although Spartan, they were safe, clean and comfortable.

'We'll go through our next move in the morning. We all need a shower and a decent sleep.'

Steve said, 'Not another night, next to this snoring bastard,' as he thumped Danny in the arm.

'Get stuffed,' said Danny.

'Meet for breakfast zero nine hundred,' continued Jack. 'And listen, when y'call home, do not talk about the diamonds. The CIA monitor everything. We don't wanna lose them now. Okay, night guys, great job these last two days. Well done.'

'Yeah, well done,' added Tom.

'Oh and errr, Tom.'

'Yes?'

'Don't forget to bring the stones in,'

Everyone laughed.

In their cabin, Jack said, 'You gonna call Helen, buddy?'

'Nah, it's after midnight in Dubai. She'll be asleep now, I'll ring in the morning.'

'Okay, you shower first, I'm gonna call Nikki.'

Jack left the cabin and sat down on the outside step and checked the time on the cell phone; the UK was three hours behind Iraq. He touched her name on the screen and put the phone to his ear. It rang twice and then,

'Hi, darling, are you ok?' she said. He could sense concern in her voice. 'I'm fine, baby, tired, but okay. We're at Safwan now.

'I had an awful dream last night; I was so worried about you, Zaikin,'

She must be worried, thought Jack. *She always calls me that if she's worried.*

'I'm safe, Nicole. No need t'worry. How was the opening?'

'Was great, but you sound so tired, Jack. Call me in the morning. Now I know your safe, you can call me in the morning. Just get some sleep.'

'Okay, night, God bless, I love you, Nikki.'

'I love you too. Sleep well.'

The phone fell silent. He looked up at the clear night sky; the full moon glowing and the big smiley face clearly definable, 'What're you grinning at?' he said to the moon.

Chapter Twenty Two
'The Weigh-in'

The dining facility was noisy and packed with about six hundred military personnel and civilian contractors. The smell of freshly brewed coffee permeated the dining area, as Castle's crew stood in line and waited to be served a cooked breakfast from the caterers manning the hot counters. Stacks of crispy bacon, sausages, beans and tomatoes, topped with fried eggs, where piled onto their plates. Then after they had helped themselves to warm bread rolls, Danish pastries and mugs of coffee, they found a table with enough seats for the group. The comfortable night's sleep and now the full English, had revived their usual good spirts, but it was the contents of the two rucksacks, that generated the excitement.

'Okay, what's the plan now, boss?' said Danny.

'Let's get breakfast over, then get back to the cabin and talk,' answered Jack.

'Everyone slept ok?' said Tom, obviously making small talk.

Pointing across the table at Danny, Steve said, 'You're bloody joking, no chance with that noisy bastard, I had to knock him out.'

'Really?' said Lisa, with surprise.

'Yeah, really,' answered Steve.

Danny looked over at Lisa and shook his head and everyone laughed.

It was a tight squeeze to get seven of them into the cabin, but using the beds and the two chairs they all managed to be seated.

'First of all, we need to be clear on the two incidents,' announced Jack. 'As you know, normally we'd report any and all contact, especially if it resulted in deaths, to military intelligence. However, considering our motive for being off grid, my first instinct is to say nothing.'

'I agree, the stones are ours, no need to advertise it,' said Steve.

'Yes, but, defending ourselves against bandits is one thing. Being pursued and engaged by an organized and motivated terrorist hit squad, leads me to the conclusion that we need to let the military know these jokers are active in Iraq.'

Tom stood up and said, 'The boss is right, we've got to report this. We got stopped by those Blackhawks and those guys will have included seeing us in their report.'

'That's right,' said Jack, 'and we told those guys we were escorting Lisa down through the river villages, that story will hold up. We say the terrorists followed us off road, into the desert. We engaged at the oasis, where one of our guys was killed.'

'That'll hold up,' said Tom, with a big smile, 'We just omit to mention the diamonds.'

'Okay, everyone good with that?' said Jack.

'Cool,' said Danny,

'No problem for me,' agreed Steve,

Ian and Santosh nodded in unison.

'Lisa?'

'It's what happened, so sure, I'm good with that story.'

Ian got up and opened the fridge, removed several bottles of water, and after passing them around said, 'So let's get down tae phase two.'

Jack swallowed some water and stood up, 'The diamonds will stay here with Tom, Danny, Steve and Santosh. I'll go to the Reserve Bank with Ian and Lisa. Let's see what kind of deal we can work out for the return of the stones.'

'And the reward,' interrupted Danny

As if speaking to a child, Jack said, 'Yes, Daniel and the reward,' which caused everyone to break into laughter.

'You better get some decent clothes first,' said Tom

'Right, we can pick up something a little more appropriate, before we meet with them,' agreed Jack, 'I'll take a couple of packets of the diamonds and a few uncut stones, to let them know we're not bullshitting. You guys sit tight here, until we get back.'

'Danny and I'll go and report the incident to the military,' said Tom. 'Santosh, can you take Vic 1 and get it cleaned please, they can't drive around Kuwait in a shitty vehicle.'

'Right, boss.'

'See if you can get hold of a decent set of weighing scales, so we know exactly how many stones we have,' continued Tom. Then to Steve, 'You stay here and guard those bags with your life, buddy,'

Steve stood to attention and snapped a smart salute, the eye patch slightly askew, 'With my life sir. Yes sir.' Again they all laughed.

'We'll be in contact soon as we have something to report. And guys, do not forget, NO mention of the diamonds on the cellphones,' added Jack. 'Those bloody Yanks listen to everything. No offence, Lisa.'

'Oh, none-taken, honey,' she said, with a wink.

Tom and Danny left the cabin to report the incident to the military. Santosh took Jack's keys and left to find the car wash and scales. Lisa returned to her cabin to check emails on her laptop. Steve, Jack and Ian remained in the cabin with the stones.

Less than an hour later Santosh returned and parked up outside the cabin in the gleaming Landcruiser. He opened the rear door and picked up a digital weighing scale.

'That was quick buddy,' said Jack.

'Yeah no problem, boss, the car wash was quiet.'

'Where'd you get the scales?' said Steve.

'The kitchens, bought 'em from a little Indian cleaner,' replied Santosh, with a grin. 'Gave him a hundred bucks.'

'A hundred bucks for weighing scales?' said Steve, 'You got ripped off.'

Santosh and Jack looked at Steve, then both looked at the two bags, stuffed with diamonds.

Steve got the point and sheepishly said, 'Err, yeah okay, nice one, Santosh.'

'Thanks, boss,' his big grin appeared again and he placed the scales on the desk.

Jack checked the scales and zeroed the digital readout, 'Okay, let's see exactly how much we got here.'

When Tom and Danny returned to the cabin, they were greeted by the rest of the team sitting in silence, looking at the two rucksacks.

'What the hell's happened?' said Tom, a clear concern in his voice.

'We just weighed the stones,' replied Jack.

Ian stood up, took a sheet a paper from the desk and handed it to Tom.

'What's this?'

'Read it,' said Jack.

'Cut, 21.853 kilos, Rough, 19.742 kilos.' said Tom, 'That's over forty kilos, not twenty.'

'Yes,' said Lisa, 'Forty one, point five nine five, actually. But uncut stones don't have the same value as cut diamonds.

'Oh no, don't tell me, we aren't billionaires,' said Danny.

Lisa continued, 'I've checked the current market value of cut and uncut and there's obviously a big difference.'

'Okay, so what is the total value?' said Tom.

'I believe, we have about one point two billion dollars, in those two bags.'

Chapter Twenty Three
'The Reserve'

The drive from the Safwan border crossing to Kuwait City was pleasant, compared to the last two days in the desert. They booked in and took three rooms in the Crowne Plaza, City Centre Hotel, only a block away from the Kuwait Reserve building.

'Let's drop these bags and meet in the foyer, in ten minutes,' said Jack. 'Then we'll go get something decent to wear.'

'Okay, see you soon,' said Lisa.

'See you in ten,' said Ian.

It was early afternoon, when the three walked into the imposing foyer of the Kuwait Reserve. Two fit looking young men, obviously security, stood each side of the ornate glass doors; their well-tailored three piece suits, belying their true function.

The larger of the two said, 'Good afternoon, sir,' as he indicated the security scanner. 'Please empty your pockets onto the tray, sir.' Jack did as instructed, then walked slowly through the scanning machine.

'Thank you, sir,' said the second man, as he offered the tray for Jack to recover his keys, cellphone, wallet and ID. The man smiled and gave a friendly nod, when he noticed the American Department of Defence badge.

But the small plastic Ziploc bag of diamonds did not seem to hold any interest for him. Lisa and Ian were invited to carry out the same process and both were given the same courteous smiles and thanks, as they completed the screening.

Two sparkling white marble columns flanked a gold and marble staircase leading from the ground floor to the mezzanine. To the left of the stairs a reception desk was manned by two beautiful Kuwaiti girls, elegantly dressed in black linen abayas.

Jack approached the reception desk, noted the nearest girl's name on her staff badge, smiled and said, 'Salam Alaikum, Good afternoon, Aliya.'

'Alaikum Salam, Good afternoon, sir,' she replied in perfect English, as she returned his smile. 'How may I help you?'

'My name is Jack Castle, this is Lisa Reynard and Mr Ian Little. We'd like to speak to a director or general manager, about a very important matter, please.'

'You obviously don't have an appointment, sir. Could you indicate what the issue concerns please?'

'No offence, Aliya, but the issue is extremely sensitive. We really do need to speak to someone at corporate level, or higher please.'

'Very good, sir, may I have a business card, please?'

Jack took out his wallet, removed a company business card and handed it to Aliya.

'Thank you, sir, if you would like to take a seat, I'll see if I can get someone to see you right away. Would you care for a drink, water, soft drink, fresh juice?'

'Water would be lovely, thank you, Aliya.'

She picked up the phone and spoke quietly into it, hung up and then made a second call. A few moments later a young Indian man came from a side room, carrying a small silver tray. He placed a linen napkin, a glass and a small bottle of water in front of each of them, nodded politely and returned to the side room.

After several minutes, the door of the lift opened and another beautiful Kuwaiti woman emerged and walked over to the three seated visitors.

'Salam Alaikum. Good afternoon. Mr Castle?'

Jack stood, smiled and said, 'Alaikum Salam, I'm, Jack Castle.'

She wore no name tag, so Jack said, 'And your name is?'

'Jamila,' she said with a smile. 'Please follow me.'

She walked to the reception desk and said, 'Visitor cards, please, Aliya.'

Jack, Lisa and Ian, were each given a small white card to fill in; once completed they returned the cards to Aliya, 'May I have your ID's please,' she said.

Jack and Ian handed their DoD badges and Lisa offered her Washington Post press card, which Aliya exchanged for visitors' cards, attached to long lanyards.

'If you would please come with me,' said Jamila, as she walked to the lift.

* * *

Back at Safwan, the guys had just finished a late lunch and were chatting about the last couple of days events, when Tom's cell phone beeped. He looked at the number and not recognizing it said, 'Tom Hillman, can I help you?'

'Mr Hillman, this is Captain Masters, we met this morning, concerning your incident yesterday.'

'Yes, captain, what can I do for you, sir?'

'Could you come to my office, please? I need to discuss something with you.'

'Sure, no problem, I'll be there shortly.'

'Thank you.'

The phone went dead. Tom stared at it, a look of concern on his face.

'What's up, Tom?' said Steve.

'Intelligence wants to talk to us again, about yesterday.'

'What for?' continued Steve.

'Fuck knows,' said Tom, 'Danny, let's go. See you guys back at the accommodation.'

* * *

Jamila knocked on the highly-polished mahogany door.

'Come in.'

She opened the door and entered in front of Jack, Ian and Lisa, then stood to the side as she introduced Jack, 'Sir, this is Mr Jack Castle and his associates.'

'Thank you, Jamila. Could you arrange some tea please.'

'Yes, sir.'

The office was quite large with half-wood-panelled walls, tasteful antique furniture and a large Persian carpet in gold and red. The floor to ceiling windows looked out over the city, with the deep blue Arabian Gulf shimmering in the distance.

'Salaam,' said the tall Kuwaiti, as he walked towards the group, his hand extended. 'My name is, Masood Bin Gassim. I am the General Director of the Reserve and I am intrigued to know what two British security men and a Washington Post journalist, have to talk to us about.'

Jack took the offered hand and shook it firmly, 'Salaam sir, I'm Jack, this is Lisa and this is Ian. And we do have something of great importance to discuss with you.'

Gassim was about the same age as Castle, slightly taller and slimmer, with bright sparkling eyes, that looked almost black in the tanned handsome face. He wore the traditional full length dish-dash, which looked as if it had just been laundered. He extended his hand towards two large, red leather Chesterfield couches, 'Please have a seat,'

They all took seats as a knock was heard, 'Come in,' said Gassim.

Another young Indian man came into the room, with a large silver tray.

'Ah, thank you, Majid.'

'You are welcome, sir,' said the man, in perfect English.

In front of each of them, he placed a linen napkin, a glass of tea, on a silver saucer, with tiny silver tea spoons. He placed a silver sugar bowl in the centre of the table, alongside a small silver salver of almond stuffed dates and delicate squares of honey filled baklava. He bowed, said, 'Thank you sir,' and left the room.

'So, to business,' said Gassim.

'First, let me thank you for meeting us, sir, without an appointment.'

Gassim made a polite gesture with his hand, as if by way of acknowledging Jack's thanks.

'May I ask, sir,' continued Jack, 'were you here at the Reserve in nineteen ninety one, when the Iraqis invaded?'

'No, I didn't take this position until late ninety eight.'

'Ah okay,' continued Jack. 'But you are aware of the atrocious way the Iraqis looted the country and specifically Kuwait City.'

'Yes, of course.' Again the polite hand gesture.

'We have been following a story of an Iraqi colonel who looted a considerable amount of diamonds from this Reserve, sir.'

'Is this what you wanted to talk to me about, a newspaper story for the Washington Post?'

'No, sir, it is far more important than that.'

'Please continue, Jack, may I call you, Jack?'

'Of course, sir. As I said, this is far more important than a news story.'

Jack took a sip from his glass and put it back on the table, leaving the saucer vacant. He removed the small plastic bag from his pocket and emptied the contents onto the saucer. The diamonds tinkled, as they trickled onto the silver saucer. He shook the saucer gently to level out the tiny pile of sparkling stones and moved the uncut ones to the side. He then slid the saucer across the table to Gassim.

'Hmmm.' said Gassim, as he picked up the saucer. 'You could have taken these to any jeweller in the diamond souk and they would have given you a fair price, Jack. We would not be interested in purchasing such a trivial amount, I'm sorry.'

'No, sir,' said Jack with a smile. 'This is just a sample. We have about forty kilos of stones, which we believe are yours. And we would like to return them to the Kuwait Reserve. For a substantial reward of course.'

Gassim almost choked as he sipped his tea. He cleared his throat and wiped his mouth with the napkin, 'Oh, please excuse me.'

'That's okay, sir, your reaction is understandable.'

'And where might these diamonds be now, Jack?'

'In a very safe place, sir.'

'Gentlemen and lady,' he said as he nodded to Lisa, 'I must speak with my colleagues about this matter.'

'Yes of course.'

'Would you be able to join us here for lunch tomorrow, say twelve thirty?'

'That would be fine, sir.'

'May I hold onto these for the time being, to let our senior appraiser look at them?'

'Of course. We'll see you tomorrow, sir.'

They all stood and Gassim shook hands with each of them in turn, he lingered over Lisa's hand for a moment longer; looked her in the eyes and said, 'It has been a pleasure to meet you.' He walked to the desk and pressed the intercom, 'Jamila, would you please show our guests out.'

* * *

Tom and Danny only had to wait a few minutes to be admitted into Captain Master's office.

'Gentlemen, good afternoon, thank you for coming, have a seat, please,'

'Thank you captain,' said Tom, 'How can we help you, sir?'

Masters moved some papers around on his desk and found what he was looking for. He picked up a folder, opened it and said, 'We sent a reconnaissance chopper to the location you gave us, ref the contact you guys had last evening.'

'Okay?'

'Your report outlined an engagement with twelve hostiles, all KIA.

'That's correct, sir.'

'One of your team also Killed in Action.' Masters looked at the report again, 'And you chose to bury his body on location.'

'Sadly, yes, sir. Ali was a local and as custom demands, we buried him before sunset. We did provide a full report, sir.'

'Yes I have that; your KIA is not the issue.'

'Okay,' said Tom, a little concern crept into his voice.

'Our recon team have reported eleven bodies, not twelve.'

'Right, so one was still alive,' interrupted Tom, 'But if he's wounded, he's not going to last long out there.'

'One would not think so. In your report you indicated four hostiles' vehicles, our team found, one burned out and two others, not four as your report says.'

'So one of these bastards, oh sorry Captain, excuse my language, has made it out?'

'No problem, *bastards* is correct,' said Masters, with a slight smile, 'Yes, looks like one hostile may have made it out.'

'Okay sir, so is there anything else you need from us?'

'No that's it, I just wanted to verify.'

'Right, thank you, captain,' said Tom, as he shook hands, 'Have a safe day, sir,'

'You, too.'

* * *

In the Crowne Plaza, Jack, Ian and Lisa, were seated in the sumptuous lounge on the first floor, having coffee and discussing the meeting with Gassim.

'Tomorrow we should know what these guys have to offer,' said Jack.

'Twenty percent is the least we'll take, right?' said Ian.

'That's the usual percentage on something like this,' confirmed Lisa.

'So we're looking at over two hundred million dollars, between seven of us?' continued Ian.

'We'll give something to Ali's family, but yeah, two hundred mil between us.'

Jack's cellphone rang; he picked it up and saw it was Tom, 'Hi, Tom, everything okay?'

'Yes and no.'

'What's up, buddy?

'We got called back to talk to Intelligence this afternoon,'

'Okay, is there a problem?'

'I don't think so, but, Captain Masters, he's the intel officer we met with, told us their recon team reported only eleven bodies on site, not twelve and one of the four vehicles is missing.'

'So one survived and made it out?'

'Sounds like it, what you think, Jack?'

'I think if he makes it to Basra and gets away, he's a lucky bastard, apart from that, what else is there to say?'

'Yeah, nothing for us to worry about I guess. How'd it go at the reserve?'

'Was good. We met with the General Director, a real smooth dude, we're meeting him and some of his directors tomorrow, for lunch.'

'Everything else okay, Tom?'

'All okay mate, talk to you tomorrow, have fun.'

'Yeah right, talk tomorrow, buddy. You be safe.'

Ian turned to Jack, 'Everything okay?'

'The military sent a recon team out to the oasis, to gather intel.'

'Yeah, that's usual, if it's safe to do so,' said Ian.

'It appears, one of the bastards made it out.'

'They were all dead, I checked the bodies at the cars.' said Ian.

'Did we check the rest?'

'I did'nae,' continued Ian, 'I was attending to, Ali.'

'Right. I guess one was only wounded and managed to get away, in one of the vehicles.'

'How'd you know that?' said Lisa.

'The recon team reported only three vehicles on site, not four.'

'But nothing for us tae worry about?'

'No, I don't think so. Ian.'

In an attempt to lighten the moment, Lisa said, 'Right gentlemen, I'm for a very large steak. Shall we go to dinner?'

Chapter Twenty Four
'Surprise'

At nine o'clock the following morning, Jack, Lisa and Ian met for breakfast. The Plaza restaurant was quite busy, with tourists, businessmen and women and offered a pleasant change from the usual bustle of a hectic, military dining facility.

'How'd you sleep, honey,' said Lisa.

'Okay, really,'

'What's the plan 'til lunchtime?' said Ian.

'Just relax, I guess. Maybe go to the pool.'

'Think I'll have a walk before it gets too hot,' said Ian.

'Okay, buddy, be back here for noon.'

'How 'bout you, Lisa?'

'I could use an hour or two, by the pool; I'll pick up a swimsuit at the store downstairs.'

'Right then, I'll see you at the pool at ten. And we'll see you downstairs at noon, Ian.'

* * *

In the centre of Basra, the small house on Imran Street looked the same as all the rest, a simple two storey building, with a roof terrace and cellar, small dirty windows, with even dirtier shutters and an old wooden door, that lead directly onto the street.

In the cellar, Massoud Kaseem had a high fever and was in a state of semi consciousness. The bullet the doctor had removed from Massoud's upper chest had not caused any damage to vital organs. He had lost a lot of blood and was extremely dehydrated, but the doctor was confident he did not have sepsis at this stage.

'Will he live, doctor?' said the old man.

'I've done all I can for the moment, brother. I must bring down the fever and rehydrate him; but he is young and strong, so there is every chance he will survive, Inshallah.'

'Inshallah,' replied the old man. 'We must know who did this and what happened to our brothers. And when we do, the infidels responsible will pay dearly.'

The old man left the cellar and went up to the roof, took out his cellphone and carefully dialled a number in Syria. The call took a few moments to go through and once connected, the quality was poor, 'Salaam Alaikum,' he said.

'Alaikum Salaam, sir.' came the reply.

'Is, *He* there?'

'Yes, sir, *He* is here.'

'Let me speak to him, please?'

A second or two later a deep, emotion less voice, said, 'Salaam,'

The old man spoke slowly, 'Salaam, sir, we have had an 'accident' in one of our factories.'

'Which one and how bad?' said deep voice.

'Southern Iraq sir and eleven of our workers have been killed.'

'My son was in charge of that contract, was he killed?'

'I am sorry, sir, yes he was.'

There was quiet on the line for several seconds and then deep voice continued, 'That was a very important contract for us, it would have enabled us to develop our company in the region.'

'Yes, sir, I know how important it was.'

'And the loss of my son,' again the line went silent for a few moments, 'It's a great loss to me and our company.'

'Yes, sir, your son,' the old man was interrupted.

'Silence, do not speak of him, you are not worthy.'

'I'm sorry sir, forgive me.'

'There will be no forgiveness for anyone, involved in this 'accident' Do you know the cause?'

'We have one worker, sir, who is badly injured, but should be well enough in a day or two, to provide a full report.'

'Very well,' continued deep voice, 'As soon as you have the cause of the accident, let me know and we will prepare an action plan, to ensure those responsible are punished.'

* * *

Jack, Lisa and Ian were escorted into the Reserve's executive dining room by Jamila.

'Mr Gassim, will be with you shortly,' she said, with a pleasant smile.

'Thank you, Jamila,' said Jack.

'This is Kamal, our restaurant manager. He will show you to your table.'

A man, in full morning dress, approached. 'Good afternoon, this way please.'

'Enjoy your lunch, good bye,' said Jamila, as she turned and left the restaurant.

They were seated at a window table, which overlooked the city, 'Would you care for some water or juice while you are waiting?' said Kamal.

'Water, please,' said Jack.

'Yes, water is fine,' said Lisa and Ian.

Ian nodded and smiled, then after Kamal had left, said, 'Only four seats. I thought we were meeting with Gassim and some of his colleagues?'

'Mmm yeah,' said Jack.

Another waiter appeared, with their water and menus.

'Strange there's no one else in the restaurant,' said Lisa.

The waiter handed out leather bound menus and said, 'The sea bass is fresh this morning.'

As the waiter left, Gassim arrived, 'Good afternoon, to you all,' and sat down on the fourth chair.

'Good afternoon, sir,' said Jack. 'So we are not meeting with anyone else?'

'No, Jack, it has been left with me, to speak with you.'

'Very well,' said Jack, with a smile, 'How do we proceed?'

'I'm afraid there is nothing to proceed with Jack, the diamonds do not belong to the Reserve.'

The three looked at each other, Jack said, 'I'm sorry, sir, I don't understand.'

'It's simple, Jack. The diamonds do not belong to us.'

'Is this some sort of joke, we're talking about a billion dollars in stones.'

'No joke, I am advised to tell you, the stones are not the property of the Kuwait Reserve and that is the end of the matter.'

'But...' Jack began to speak and was silenced by Gassim's raised hand.

'No need to ask further questions, Jack, the matter is closed. Now if you will excuse me, I have other business to attend to. Please stay and enjoy your lunch.'

He stood up and took a small cloth pouch from his pocket, opened it and poured the contents onto Jack's side plate, 'And don't forget these. Goodbye and good luck to you all.'

'What the hell just happened?' said Lisa.

Chapter Twenty Five
'The Diamond Souk'

They walked back to the Crowne Plaza in stunned silence. The temperature was in the low forties centigrade and the street was busy with traffic. It was only a short walk, from the Reserve to the hotel, but they were sweating profusely, as they entered the foyer. The chill of the air conditioning was a welcome relief, from the searing heat of the afternoon.

Once in the lounge and with water and soft drinks in front of them, Jack said, 'There's something seriously wrong here, and I don't understand what. Why would they not want to have their diamonds returned?'

'Beats me,' said Ian.

'Unless there's something wrong with them?' said Lisa.

'What'd you mean?' said Ian, 'What the hell could be wrong with diamonds, unless they're fake?'

'They can't be fake,' said Jack, 'Can they?'

'There's one way to find out,' said Lisa.

'You're right,' continued Jack, 'So let's go see, if there is anything wrong with em.'

'How?' said Ian.

Jack dropped the cloth pouch on to the table and said, 'We do as that tosser Gassim said and take these to the diamond souk.'

'Shouldn't we let the guys know?' said Ian.

'Let's see what we find out at the diamond souk, first. Then we'll head back to Safwan and decide on our next move.'

The Kuwait Diamond Souk is the Hatton Garden of the Middle East and, contrary to popular belief, is not overrun by Dutch, Jewish or South African stores. The majority of the traders, both wholesale and retail, are Indian; indeed the west coast of India cuts and polishes more diamonds than anywhere else in the world.

It was late afternoon when the three took the local taxi to the souk. The temperature had dropped a little, but was still extremely unpleasant with the hot wind coming in off the desert. The souk was bustling with tourists, locals and traders, each there to buy or sell precious stones of all kinds. Every shop they passed had an Indian outside touting for business. Each tout had the same spiel, 'Diamonds, rubies, emeralds, sapphires, come in sir, bring madam. Buy her diamond here.'

Jack was looking for a small shop with a workshop in the rear, so they could actually keep an eye on the gemmologist, when the stones were inspected.

'How about this place?' said Ian.

The small shop had only one customer, the tiny work area at the rear was manned by a very old Indian man, hunched over a small grinding wheel.

'Yeah, this will do,' said Jack.

They had a problem to squeeze into the tiny shop area, but the single customer decided not to purchase the stone he was scrutinizing, and left; giving just enough room for the three to stand in front of the small counter.

'Good afternoon,' said Jack.

'Good afternoon, sir, how may I help you?' said the smart middle-aged Indian assistant.

'We need to have some diamonds appraised, please.

'Certainly, sir, my father can look at your stones now, excuse me for a second.'

The assistant went to the rear and tapped the old man on the shoulder, then spoke in a loud voice, 'Father, these people need an appraisal please.'

The old man nodded, continued working for a few seconds and then switched off the grinding wheel.

'He is almost deaf, so you will have to speak up, when you talk to him, sir.'

'Thank you,' said Jack, with a nod and a smile.

'Can I get you some water?'

'Oh that would be great, thank you.'

The assistant went into the rear of the shop and returned with three small bottles of water and handed them out. The old man hobbled to the counter and said in a soft voice, 'Good afternoon, sir.'

'Good afternoon,' said Jack in a raised voice, 'As we told your son, we need to have some stones appraised please, is that possible?'

'Of course, of course,' said the old man, a smile on his craggy face.

He indicated to his son to shut the door and display the closed sign. Jack took the pouch from his pocket and poured the stones onto a small, felt covered tray, the cut stones mixed with the uncut. The old man put on a pair of spectacles, but instead of the normal lenses, the frames had a built-in loupe, enabling the wearer to examine the stones, without having to hold the loupe to the eye. He took a delicate pair of tweezers and separated the cut from the rough, then picked up several of the cut stones, nodding each time, 'These are very fine stones,' he said with a smile, his eyes sparkled in obvious appreciation for the beautiful pieces of carbon.

'They are medium to high clarity and elegantly cut, to achieve maximum value. They are beautiful diamonds, sir,'

'That's good, that's good,' said Jack.

Ian and Lisa both noted the air of relief in Jack's voice.

'What about the uncut stones, can you tell me anything about them, please?'

'I will need to do a couple of tests; it will not take too long. Can you wait, sir?'

'Please do what you have to.'

The old man picked up the five large uncut stones and took them back to his tiny work bench. Jack watched as he filed a small amount from each stone in turn, then placed the filings onto tiny microscope slides. He then viewed each slide under an antique microscope. When he had viewed all the slides, he turned and looked at Jack. The look felt strange to Jack and it appeared the old man's mood had changed from excitement at seeing the diamonds, to concern about the rough stones.

'Anything wrong?' said Jack, almost shouting.

The old man held up his hand and took down a small bottle of liquid, from the cluttered work shelf above his bench. He filed a little more off each of the stones and placed the filings into tiny shallow bowls. Then, taking a small pipette, he placed a single drop of the liquid, into each of the five bowls. He turned to Jack and gave him the strange look again. He turned back to the task in hand and placed the loupe spectacles back on, as he studied each of the tiny bowls in turn.

Once finished with his tests, the old man picked up the five uncut stones and returned to the counter, looked at Jack and said, 'These stones will become fine diamonds, after they are cut and polished, sir.'

'Oh that's great news,' said Jack, again with clear relief in his voice.

'May I ask where you acquired them, sir?'

'They were taken in payment for some work my company did.'

'Do you know where the uncut stones originated, sir?' said the old man.

'No I don't. You can tell their origin?'

'Yes, sir, the test I completed, confirmed they were good quality stones and they will produce excellent diamonds. The test also confirmed the region, they were mined from.'

'Right and where was that?'

'They were mined in the central African belt, Sierra Leone, Congo, Liberia, those locations.'

'Conflict stones,' said Lisa, 'Blood diamonds.'

'Yes,' said the old man, 'But still very valuable.'

'Okay,' said Jack, 'Thank you for your time, sir and your excellent appraisal. What do we owe you?'

'Whatever you wish, sir. A few dinars will be fine.' said the old man, the smile back on his craggy face.

Jack had almost finished returning the stones to the pouch and had one uncut stone, about the size of a broad bean, in his fingers; he placed the stone back on the tray. He shook hands with the old man and his son and said, 'Thank you very much indeed.'

'Sir, this is far too much, we cannot take this,' said the old man.

'We've had good fortune with these,' said Jack, as he shook the pouch, 'You can enjoy some of our fortune as well.'

'Thank you, sir. God bless you.'

Chapter Twenty Six
'New Plan'

They left the shop and made their way through the crowded souk, back to the main road. Ian hailed a taxi from the nearby rank and they climbed into the welcome air-conditioned vehicle.

'So, blood diamonds,' said Lisa quietly.

'Yeah,' said Jack, 'And obviously that's why the Reserve didn't want to claim ownership.'

'But it's over a billion dollars, they're just throwing away,' said Ian.

'Do you think they really need a billion?' said Jack, 'That's small change to the Kuwaitis.'

'And very bad publicity, if they were to acknowledge they handled conflict stones.'

'But we did nae know they were conflict diamonds 'til now.' said Ian.

'Yes, but the Reserve didn't know that, honey.'

'That's right. Okay, we know we have a load of diamonds that are worth a fortune' said Jack,

'But what do we do with them?'

'Can we no just sell them ourselves?' said Ian.

'It's not that easy to sell forty kilos of diamonds,' answered Lisa.

'No, it's not. That's why taking a reward was an elegant solution.'

'So what now?' said Ian.

'I think I may have an idea,' said Jack, with a grin, 'Let's check-out and get back to Safwan and discuss it with the guys.'

'Aw do we have tae go back? Can we no get another night in a decent hotel?' moaned Ian.

'When we get rid of these stones buddy, you can spend the rest of your life in a decent hotel.'

They pulled into the accommodation area at Safwan, just after ten. The moon was still full and the temperature had dropped to a bearable thirty degrees. Tom and the rest of the crew were waiting for them, as they arrived.

'Get a load of this,' said Danny, as he felt the lapel of Ian's linen suit, 'Very stylish.'

'Hi, mate how you doing?' said Tom.

'Okay, buddy, we're good,' said Jack. 'Let's get inside and have a chat.'

They all piled into the cabin and took seats on beds and chairs, their faces clearly excited at the return of Jack and the prospect of handing over the diamonds, for a huge reward.

'Okay, bad news first,' said Jack.

'Oh fuck,' said Danny.

'Shut it,' said Steve, as he gave his friend a dig in the arm.

'As I was saying, before being so rudely interrupted,' said Jack with feigned indignation.

'The Kuwaiti Reserve, are not interested in the stones.'

'What the…?' said Steve, as Jack held his hand up.

'Hold on, let me finish.'

'Sorry, boss.'

'They said the stones were not their property and had no interest in them.'

'We thought, they maybe were fake,' added Ian.

'Oh shit, no,' said Danny.

'Will you shut the fuck up!' said Steve.

'So we took the stones to the diamond souk and had them appraised.' continued Jack.

'And?' said Danny.

'The diamonds are apparently excellent quality. The uncut stones are also worth a fortune.'

'So, what's the problem?' said Steve.

'Problem is, the uncut stones are from central Africa.'

'What does that mean, boss?' said Santosh.

'Means they're from conflict zones, blood diamonds,' said Lisa.

'Okay,' said Danny, 'We have a bag full of diamonds, let's just sell them. We still get to make a fortune and we just bin the uncut?'

'Problem is, who do we sell them too?' said Tom.

'Ah, now that's the good news,' said Jack, 'I may have a solution, but I need to make a call first.'

'So make the call, f'fuck sake,' said Danny.

Jack left the cabin and sat on the outside step, took the cellphone from his pocket and pressed Nicole's number.

'Zaikin, how are you darling?'

'Hi, baby, I'm fine, back in Safwan. It's great to hear your voice, how you doing?'

'I'm good, busy, busy, busy.'

'Yeah, same as always, Nikki. Listen darling, you know I'm working on something big here.'

'Yes.'

'Well, I need some serious help.'

'What can I do?'

'Is, Dimitri in Abu Dhabi?'

'Yes, I spoke with him earlier today. He's just got back from Japan.'

'Okay, good. I need to meet with him urgently. Can you call him please? Let him know I am coming to Abu Dhabi and if possible, can I see him tomorrow?'

'Yes, darling, I'll call him right away.'

'And, Nicole, I need you to come to AD as well.'

'Okay, all sounds very mysterious and exciting. I'll see if I can get a flight out in the morning.'

'Thanks, Nikki, I need to get back to the guys. I'll talk soon, I love you baby.'

'I love you, too, darling. Night, God bless.'

Jack considered his plan for a few more seconds and then stood up and went back into the crowded cabin.

'Okay mate, what's the plan?' said Tom.

'There's only one guy I know who can help us with the stones now. Either buy them or trade them.'

'And who might that be?' said Lisa.

'Dimitri,' said Jack, with a big smile.

'Yes, right, Dimitri,' said Tom with obvious delight.

'Sorry boys, but who is Dimitri?' said Lisa.

'Dimitri Mikhailovich Orlov,' said Tom.

'Nicole's father,' said Jack.

Just then Jack's cellphone beeped, he took it out and pressed the accept, 'Hi, baby.'

'Hi, darling, I just spoke with Dad. He's okay for tomorrow. He said if you let him know what time your plane arrives, he'll send Mike to pick you up and take you to the island.'

'Oh that's great, thank you darling, good night.'

'Night, Jack, love you.'

'You, too, baby.'

'Nicole's just spoken to Dimitri. I'm going to meet him in Abu Dhabi tomorrow. Ian, can you get online, book me a flight please?'

'Nae bother, I'll get on it right now, boss,' he said, and left the cabin.

The atmosphere in the room had changed and returned to the earlier excited expectation.

'Just a second,' said Lisa, 'Dimitri Orlov, the Russian industrialist, is your father in law?'

'Well he's not my father in law, but I've known him ever since I met Nicole, over fifteen years ago. We get on very well.'

'He has an island, off the coast of Abu Dhabi, Orel Island.' said Lisa.

'That's right, Orel, is Russian for eagle,' said Jack.

'Well, that's the new plan, guys,' said Tom, then turning to Jack said, 'Nice one mate.'

Danny, Steve and Santosh left the cabin, clearly excited about the new plan. 'Lisa, I'm gonna get a shower, then go get something to eat, how about you?' said Jack.

'We've had nothing since breakfast, so yeah, I could eat something.'

'Okay, see you back here, in about thirty minutes?'

'Sure, honey, see you then.'

Jack showered quickly and changed into his usual chinos and polo shirt, then went back into the bedroom. Tom lay on his bed watching the news, on TV.

'So it turned a bit tricky at the Reserve, mate?'

'Yeah, the guy we met, Gassim, seemed keen as mustard, when we first saw him. But the next day he was not interested. Obviously someone at the Reserve knew about the conflict stones.'

'So, do you think, Dimitri will buy them?'

'He has many fingers in many pies. I'm sure he'll be interested.'

There was a knock on the door and Jack shouted, 'Come in'

'Ready?' said Lisa.

'Yeah, you coming, Tom?'

'No, thanks, we ate earlier.'

'Okay, see you soon, won't be too late.'

'No problem.'

He checked his Rolex, it was almost eleven o'clock, the temperature had dropped, but was still in the high twenties. 'Shall we walk over?'

'Sure honey, I don't mind.'

The coffee shop was not too busy and they didn't have to wait to get served. They took chicken sandwiches, french fries and fruit juice and found a table in the corner of the room.

* * *

The small farm was located on the outskirts of Baghdad. Anyone passing, or visiting the place, would see the normal olive groves and fig trees, a few goats and poultry. The farmhouse, work sheds and outbuildings were in reasonable repair and to all intents and purposes it resembled any other farm in the vicinity.

In the warm night air, two men sat cross-legged, on the flat roof of the house. The younger, in his late twenties, listened intently to the other, much older man. He spoke in a deep emotionless voice, a voice that once heard was never forgotten, a voice so calm, yet so ominous, the listener was compelled to obey his every word.

'Jamal, I have made the journey here from Syria, at great personal risk. I hope you have something to tell me, about your brother's failed mission?'

'Yes, father.'

'Have you discovered who was responsible for his death?'

'We believe so, father. When my brother, Salim met with the intermediary....'

'This, Ali Wassam?'

'Yes, father, Ali Wassam. He told Salim of the infidels plans, to recover a vast amount of diamonds from the southern desert.'

'Jamal, I am aware of the plan, I want to know who was responsible, for killing my son, your older brother.'

'Yes, father. Ali Wassam said the leader of the infidel group, is a man called Jack Castle.'

'Go on.'

'Jack Castle is partner, in the security company he operates in Baghdad. The other partner is a man called Adil Mubarak, who lives in Dubai.'

'Anything else?'

'That is all we have for the moment, father.'

'Tomorrow morning, you will go to Dubai and question Mubarak. Discover everything about this, Jack Castle. If he has a wife, children, mother, father. When you have this information, you will visit Jack Castle and take everything from him; everything he holds dear, including the diamonds.'

'Inshallah, father, Inshallah.'

Chapter Twenty Seven
'Down to AD'

The drop off area at the airport was choked with taxis and local vehicles and backed up all the way down the approach ramp.

'Better jump out here, boss and walk up the ramp,' said Santosh.

'Yeah, right, okay, thanks, buddy. I'll be in touch. Be safe.'

Jack got out of the Landcruiser and as he leaned in to shake Santosh's hand, a big Mercedes limo beeped its horn behind them.

'Okay, boss, see you soon, good luck.' The big Santosh smile was flashed as Jack closed the door. He turned and raised a hand in apology to the limo behind, then walked quickly up the ramp and into the hectic departures concourse and the welcome relief of the cool air-conditioning. His flight departed in an hour, so he went straight to check-in and security. Once at the gate he checked his cellphone and noticed a text from Nicole, *[On Etihad 08:00. Heathrow – AD. eta 19:00 xxx]* he smiled and typed in *[see you tonight- luv you xxx]*. He thought for a moment and then dialled his business partner in Dubai, the phone rang for a few seconds.

'Hello, Jack, everything okay, my friend?'

'Hi, Adil, everything's good. I'm just calling to say I'm on my way to Orel Island, I have some business with, Dimitri.'

'Ah, okay, how long will you be down here?'

'A few days at least, Nicole is flying in tomorrow. So once we get our business finalised, maybe you and Layla can come down as well?'

'Oh, that is very kind, thank you Jack. You know how Layla loves the island.'

'Ok, buddy, I have to go, bye for now, love to Layla.'

'Bye, Jack, take care.'

The flight to Abu Dhabi was crowded with business people, locals and groups of Asian workers in transit back to the sub-continent. He looked out the window at the Arabian Gulf below. He could clearly see the wake of several ships travelling in all directions, the oil rigs, their flares burning golden, against the azure of the gulf. The feeling of well-being at leaving Iraq brought a smile to his face. Then he thought of Nicole. She would be in the air now and the prospect of being with her again, after so many weeks away, aroused him and he smiled again.

The plane landed on time and as Jack stepped out of the aircraft and onto the steps, the heat hit him like a sledgehammer, after the chill of the cabin. He saw a large white BMW courtesy car parked, white a uniformed driver standing next to it. When the driver saw Jack, he walked to the bottom of the steps.

'Good afternoon, sir. Mr Castle?' said the driver.

'Hi there, yes, Jack Castle.'

'This way please, sir.'

The engine was running and the vehicle was pleasantly cool. Jack settled into the back seat, looked around and said, 'Gimme a Jaguar any day.'

'I'm sorry, sir, did you say something?'

'No nothing, son. Just thinking out loud.'

The driver took the vehicle round the outside of the main runway and across the other side of the airport, to the private aviation and VIP area. The car pulled up in front of a very smart building with a pretty local girl in uniform, waiting outside.

'Mr Castle, sir?'

'Yes, hello.'

'Welcome to Abu Dhabi sir, my name is, Mina. This way please.'

Jack nodded to the driver and said, 'Thank you.'

Inside, he handed over his passport and took a seat in the reception area. He was offered water, fruit juice, stuffed dates and a cool face cloth. He picked up the face cloth and water, smiling as he did so. Mina returned with the passport, 'If you would like to come with me, sir, your flight is ready to leave.'

'Great.'

They walked back outside and the same BMW was waiting. The driver stood by the rear door and held it open.

'Hello again, sir,' said the driver, with a smile.

'Have an enjoyable flight, Mr Castle.'

'Thank you, Mina, bye.'

The BMW drove a few hundred metres, to the private helipad and pulled up alongside a sleek shiny black executive helicopter, with Dimitri's corporate logo, the eagles head, emblazoned on the fuselage. The driver opened the car door and said, 'Have a safe flight, sir.'

'Thank you again,' said Jack.

The pilot stood next to the open door of the chopper and said, 'Good afternoon, Mr Castle, nice to see you again, sir.'

'Good to see you, too, Mike.'

Jack climbed into the luxurious seats, strapped in and put the headphones on. The level of luxury impressed him and nowadays it took a lot to do that; Dimitri did not do anything by halves, he thought. There was a small concealed cool box in the armrest and he helped himself to a can of Red Bull, specially stocked for him by the pilot. As Mike climbed in, Jack raised the can and said, 'Thanks, Mike, much appreciated.'

'You're welcome, sir.'

The pilot strapped in and efficiently went through the pre-flight checks, then spoke into the microphone, 'Eagle six seven one, request clearance please.'

A pleasant voice came back and said, 'Eagle six seven one, you are clear to proceed.'

'Copy that, thank you control.'

The rotors began to spin and gain momentum, the helicopter vibrated slightly, as the revolutions built and then stabilized, as the rear of the aircraft lifted. The rotors were now a blur, as the helicopter lifted off and climbed slowly, into the hot afternoon air. They flew at one thousand feet while over the city, but once out over the gulf, Mike dropped to five hundred feet. He knew Jack enjoyed flying, especially low flying and the approach to the island was even more spectacular, when made at low level.

'There it is,' said Jack into the microphone, 'Orel Island!'

He loved coming here with Nicole. The peace and calm the island provided, far outweighed the luxury and opulence. He remembered the first time he and Nicole had come here. They had stayed in the mansion and despite its unashamed luxury and elegance, it seemed imposing and cold. Nicole had sensed his reluctance at being in the mansion, so they had moved to one of the guest villas on the beach and it was there, they really made the most of being together. Now every time they visited the island, they always stayed in the same villa.

'Orel Island, this is eagle six seven one, permission to land.'

Jack was pulled from his reminiscence, at the sound of Mike's voice.

'Please check your seat belt, Mr Castle, going in now, sir.'

The pilot banked the aircraft to the right and increased speed, as the agile helicopter circled Orel, then slowed and hovered, as it approached the small landing pad, at the tip of the island.

'Eagle six seven one, clear to land.'

'Roger, Orel, thank you.'

Chapter Twenty Eight
'Orel Island'

Dimitri was waiting in the small service building, adjacent to the helipad and as Jack disembarked the aircraft, came out to welcome him.

'Good to see you again, my boy,' he said, with a genuine smile on his face.

Dimitri was only fifteen years older than Jack, but he always referred to him affectionately as 'my boy'. They shook hands, hugged and Jack said, 'It's really great to see you again, Mitri.'

He used the abbreviated version of Dimitri, as is customary in Russia, between family and close friends.

'You're looking very well indeed, Mitri.'

'I'm good, Jack, I'm so happy to have you and Nicole here again.'

'Yes, she's arriving at seven this evening,'

'I know, I've arrange to have her picked up already. Okay let's get up to the house.'

A very smart golf buggy, in black and gold, with the eagle's head logo on the front, was parked at the side of the service building and with a wave of his hand, the old Russian indicated to the driver's seat, and said, 'You drive, Jack.'

Orel Island, was one of several manmade islands the Abu Dhabi government had constructed a few kilometres offshore. The intention was for independent companies to buy the islands and develop them, but Dimitri, had not wished to share his island with anyone and had bought the whole crescent shaped property, several years ago, for an undisclosed sum. In the centre of the crescent stood the mansion, each side of the big house, stood two large villas and towards each curve of the crescent stood six smaller bungalows, all the properties overlooked the bay and had direct access to the beach.

Such was Dimitri's love of everything British he had designed and built the 'mansion' as an English country house. The villas and bungalows were all built in the contemporary style and although the mansion looked somewhat incongruous, the understated elegance worked. There were smaller accommodation buildings at the rear of the property for staff, as well as generators and service buildings. One end of the crescent housed the helipad and small service building, while the other provided shelter for a small marina. Five kilometres away, on the mainland, Dimitri had a second property that accommodated another helipad and service hanger. There was a small marina, with a couple of shuttle boats and a medium sized yacht. A large garage and maintenance facility, housed his Bentley Continental, E Type Jaguar and three Range Rovers.

Dimitri and Jack pulled up at the front of the mansion and entered the classically English foyer; the cool air inside supplied by the best air-conditioning system money could buy.

'Let's go into the study,' said Dimitri, 'I'm sure you want to get straight to business?'

The large study was tastefully decorated and adorned with several antiques and paintings.

A large Adam fireplace stood imposingly at the rear of the room and next to the windows, a large mahogany desk, which reputedly once belonged to Winston Churchill. The most striking feature in the study was the life size painting above the fireplace; which looked just like Nicole, but in fact, was her mother, Elizabeth.

Jack loved this room, he always imagined if he ever retired, this would be the kind of place he would like to spend his years in, reading, writing, remembering, with Nicole at his side. A sudden feeling of joy came over him at the thought of being with her that evening; where ever he went, she was always in his head and heart and as the years had gone on, it was more and more difficult to be away from her.

'Would you like a drink, Jack?'

'Some water, please.'

Dimitri turned, pushed a small button on the wall and a large panel swung slowly open, revealing a fully stocked bar, 'Nothing stronger?'

'No thanks, water is fine.'

'Let's have a seat over here,' said Dimitri, indicating two padded leather club chairs.

'Now Jack, tell me what's going on.'

* * *

Jamal handed her phone to the woman and said, 'Tell your husband to come home now. Tell him it's important. Do not say anything else.'

She took the smart phone and pressed Adil's name on the screen, a few seconds later he answered, 'Hello, Layla.'

She tried to keep the fear from her voice and spoke quietly, 'Adil, can you come home now please, it's important.'

'What's wrong?'

'Just please come home. Right now, Adil, it is very important.'

'Okay, I'll be there in thirty minutes.'

The man took the phone from her. 'Well done, now that wasn't too bad was it?'

The other man said, 'Please sit here, Layla,' as he pointed to an upright chair with wooden arms.

'May I call you Layla? I am Jamal,' he said with an emotionless smile.

'What is it you want? We have money in the safe; I can open it for you.'

'That's very kind Layla, but we are not here for money. Let's just wait until you husband arrives.'

As she sat in the chair, the second man placed her hands on the wooden arms. Then opened his small rucksack and removed a roll of gaffer tape, which he used to secure her arms to the chair. Kneeling down he spread her legs and secured her ankles to the chair legs, then tore a short strip off and pressed it over her mouth. He returned the tape to the rucksack and took out a small, automatic pistol with a silencer; placed it on the ornate marble table at her side and said, 'Now we just need to wait for, Adil.'

* * *

Jack had talked for about an hour, Dimitri asked the occasional question, but in the main, let Jack go through the whole story, from the Iraqi colonel, right up to discovering that half the stones were blood diamonds.

'Interesting story, Jack. Moladitz,' said, Dimitri, slipping into his native tongue. 'Well done, well done indeed, on recovering the diamonds.'

'It wasn't as easy as it sounded, Mitri. We did have a couple of incidents on the way.'

'I'm sure, but you and your men are safe. And the stones are with them at Safwan?'

'Yes.'

'So you need my help, to get the stones out of Kuwait?'

'That's the first priority. The next question is, can you buy them or broker them for us?'

'I can do anything, Jack, but first let's get the stones here, shall we?'

He went to the big desk, touched the screen on a very high tech intercom system and said, 'Olga, can you come in please.'

Jack smiled to himself as Olga's name was mentioned. She had been Dimitri's PA, for about ten years and as he had got older, she had assumed a secondary role as his nurse. Olga was an exceptionally intelligent woman, who had great experience in business and, at the request of Dimitri, had undergone intensive training to qualify as a registered nurse. It was clear she not only had great respect for the man, but had great affection as well. Whether or not there was anything more to the relationship, was known only to Olga and Dimitri.

There was a firm knock on the door. 'Come in, Olga.'

Jack watched her walk across to the big desk. She would be about forty years old now, very elegant, tall, dark hair, lovely face, and great figure. It wasn't just her skills, which had kept her with him for so many years.

'Yes, sir, what can I do for you?'

Jack stood and moved towards her, his hand extended. 'Hello, Olga, lovely to see you again.'

'Hello, yes it's good to see you, too, and Nicole arrives this evening. We are all thrilled.'

Turning to her boss, she said again, 'Sir?'

'Can you get onto the Russian Embassy, please, speak with the Ambassador. Ask him if he could give me a call on my private number. When he's free of course.'

'Yes, sir.'

Jack watched as she walked back to the door; then looked at Dimitri, the faint smile just perceptible on the old man's face.

* * *

The Mercedes entered the gates and stopped outside the front door. Adil Mubarak left the vehicle and rushed into the villa. 'Layla, I'm back. What's the matter?'

As he entered the large sitting room, he was stunned to see his wife bound to the armchair, the two men each side of her and the gun on the table. She had been strong up until now, but when she saw her husband, she began to sob, tears ran down her face and her shoulders moved uncontrollably, as the sobs deepened.

'What do you want? Do you want money, there is money here. Take anything you want,' his words just blurted out, his eyes fixed on his lovely wife. He moved towards her and one of the men stood in front of her.

'Salaam, brother, my name is Jamal.'

'I am not your brother, if I were, you wouldn't be doing this. What do you want?'

'Sit down, Adil, may I call you, Adil?'

The second man picked up the gun and stood behind Layla.

'I am going to ask you several questions, Adil. For each question you fail to answer, or if I think you are lying, the lovely Layla here will suffer. Do you understand?'

Adil was stunned. He said nothing, then Jamal slapped him across the face, 'Focus, Adil, answer my questions and no one will be hurt. Do you understand?'

Adil nodded, his gaze never left Layla. They both had tears in their eyes.

'Your business partner is, Jack Castle?'

Adil looked at the man, 'Jack Castle, this is about, Jack?'

The man behind Layla put the muzzle of the silencer, onto the back of her hand, 'Wait. Wait. Yes, yes, Jack is my partner.'

'Good, see how easy that was and no one is hurt.' said Jamal.

'I need to know, everything about Mr Castle, his family, his friends, his location. Once I have the answers to my questions, we will leave.'

Chapter Twenty Nine
'Diplomatic Bag'

In less than ten minutes, after asking Olga to call the Embassy, Dimitri's smart phone came to life with the Russian national anthem, ring tone. Jack smiled as Mitri picked up the phone, checked the screen and said, 'Ah, here we go. Mr Ambassador, thank you for taking the time to call. Yes I'm fine, how the hell are you doing, Sergey?' Dimitri laughed out loud, at what was obviously a private joke. Jack knew Dimitri and Sergey were great friends and went way back to the Ambassador's days as a minor secretary in the Politburo.

'Sergey, I need a small favour please.'

After several minutes and a lot more laughter, Dimitri closed the call. 'Okay let me get Olga back in.'

He pressed the hi-tech intercom again, 'Olga, come in please.'

A few seconds later, came the firm knock on the door. 'Come in.'

'Yes, sir?'

'Have a seat, please,'

'Thank you, sir.'

'I've just spoken with the Ambassador and he'll help us with a small problem we have.'

'Yes, sir.'

'Jack will give you the names of his men, they need to be brought from Kuwait to Orel. They have some sensitive material with them, which must be transported via the 'diplomatic bag'. The Embassy will provide all relevant documentation.'

'Understood, sir. I take it this needs to happen immediately.'

'Yes, please and also get onto the pilot; let him know to pick up...' he looked at Jack and said, 'Jack, how many of your guys?'

'Six, I'll call Tom now and have him email passport copies right away, Olga.'

'Thanks, Jack.'

She turned to Dimitri, 'Anything else sir?'

'No, I think that's it for now.'

'Very good, sir, excuse me.'

'Thank you, Olga.'

Jack looked at his Rolex, it was just after three. 'I think I'll go and get a shower, Mitri. There's not much else we can do just yet, is there?'

'Sure, Jack, I'll get a couple of my gemmologists, over from India. If there's over forty kilos of stones, it will take a while to appraise and value the diamonds and assess the un-cuts.'

'Okay, good. When do you think my guys will get here?'

'The Embassy is good, but I doubt we will get the documentation until later today, so best we can expect is the guys to arrive mid-morning tomorrow.'

'That's good, means I'll be able to have an evening with Nikki, without the wild bunch hanging around.'

Dimitri laughed, 'Yes, we can have dinner here and then you two can get off down to your villa later.'

'Sounds great, Mitri, thanks, I'll see you later. Okay if I go to the airport to meet, Nikki?'

'Of course. I'll get, Olga to let Mike know you'll be on-board.'

Jack left the mansion and took one of the buggies down to his villa. The door was unlocked and the air-conditioning had chilled the building nicely. One of the housekeepers was placing several vases of fresh flowers around the place and Jack startled her when he said, 'Hello'

'Oh, hello, sir, I will be finished in a moment.'

'No problem, lovely flowers. Nicole will love them, thank you.'

'My pleasure, sir, these are her favourites.'

'Yes I know,' he said with a smile.

He went through to the bedroom, dropped his bag on the bed and heard the housekeeper call, 'That's it, sir. I have finished, good afternoon.'

'Thank you,' he shouted back.

He took out the cellphone and called Tom.

'Hi, mate, how's it going in the land of luxury?'

'Hi, Tom, oh it's a struggle here, don't know how I can put up with it.'

They both laughed and Jack said, 'Okay, here's the plan. Dimitri will send his plane to pick you lot up in the morning, not sure what the departure time is, but Olga will mail you with flight information.'

'How is the lovely, Olga?'

'Still a knockout,' said Jack, 'But devoted to her job, so calm down.'

'Devoted to, Dimitri more like. Are you sure you want us all down there?

'Yes. It's okay with Dimitri and everyone has an interest in the diamonds, so why not?'

'Just a bit upmarket for this bunch, isn't it?'

They laughed again and Jack continued, 'Dimitri has spoken to the Russian Ambassador and he's arranging a diplomatic bag for the stones, so no problems with customs in Kuwait or Abu Dhabi.'

'Oh, that's cool. Nice one mate.'

'Not me. Dimitri. He and the ambassador are old pals.'

'Why does that not surprise me?'

'I'm going to text you Olga's email address now. Send her the guys' passport copies, please.'

'What about Lisa?'

'Yes, hers as well, Tom. She's part of the team.'

'Okay, no problem. Is that it?'

'That's it for now. I'll see you in the morning, Tom. Be safe.'

Jack threw the cellphone onto the bed, stripped off and went into the bathroom. After he had shaved and showered, he wrapped a towel around his waist and walked out onto the veranda. He had been to the island many times over the years, but each time he returned he never failed to be impressed by the way Dimitri had developed and turned a manmade strip of sand, into such a beautifully natural island. He went back inside, closed the big glass doors and lay down on the bed.

He was startled awake by the beep of the house phone. 'Hello?' he said, in a sleepy voice.

'Hello, Jack, the helicopter will be leaving in thirty minutes, if you would care to go down to the helipad, when you're ready please.'

'Okay, thank you, Olga.'

'Do you need me to send a buggy for you?'

'No, its fine, I have one here.'

'Okay, have a good flight. See you and Nicole later.'

Chapter Thirty
'Nicole'

The Etihad flight was delayed by thirty minutes, so Jack waited in the private lounge for Nicole's plane to arrive. He chatted to the same pretty girls who attended to him earlier in the day. He was eager to see Nicole and the excitement of being with her after so many weeks was building.

'The Heathrow flight has just landed, sir,' said one of the girls.

'Thank you,' he said with a smile.

He stood up and went to the front of the lounge, better to watch for the courtesy car. An endless ten minutes passed, then he saw the BMW come round the end of the main runway, towards the private aviation area. He stepped outside and after the chill of the lounge, the warm evening air felt a lot hotter than it was. One of his greatest pleasures, every time he met Nicole; in an airport or railway station; was to watch her walk towards him. At times it almost took his breath away, when he saw her beautiful face and heart melting smile. He truly loved this woman.

The BMW pulled up in front of him, the black tinted windows obscuring the interior. The driver quickly jumped out and went to the back door and opened it. She stepped out, looked at Jack and there it was, the smile in a million.

'Zaikin,' was all she could get out, before he had her in his arms. His mouth on hers, briefly, not long enough, he drew back and looked into the beautiful eyes.

'Nikki, it's wonderful to see you, darling.'

They walked back into the lounge and the pretty attendant took her passport.

'I love you in this outfit,' he said, as he stepped back, better to enjoy the view.

'I know you do, darling.'

'And you've cut your hair and coloured it a little.'

'Yes. You like it?'

'Love it,' he said, then kissed her again.

The girl returned with Nicole's passport and they walked back outside, to the waiting courtesy car. A few moments later they pulled up alongside the helicopter; with Mike standing at the open door. The driver opened Nicole's door, as Jack jumped out and opened the boot to collect her luggage.

'Lovely to see you again, Miss Nicole,' said Mike.

'Thank you, Mike, it's great to be back.'

The driver quickly took the luggage from Jack and, under the supervision of the pilot, loaded it into the stowage compartment, at the side of the fuselage.

'Good evening, madam, sir,' said the driver.

Nicole turned and said, 'Thank you,' then climbed into the cabin, as Jack enjoyed the view of the tight pants over her perfect bottom, resisting the urge to slap it, mumbled, 'Hmmm, nice bum chief!'

As she sat down, she saw his smile, 'I heard that! Behave.'

He climbed in beside her, kissed her and said, 'Never.'

The door was closed and the air-conditioning quickly took the temperature down to a pleasant twenty centigrade. He leaned across, touched her face and said, 'I'm so happy to see you,' then kissed her again.

Dimitri was waiting at the helipad service building and excited at the thought of seeing his daughter again. He had seen her in London a few weeks ago, but she had not been to the island for about six months. The sun was going down and the temperature had dropped, but was still in the low thirties. He heard the flight controller give the 'all clear to land' and saw the chopper circle the end of the island and become silhouetted in the rays of the setting sun.

The helicopter touched down gently and as the rotors stopped Dimitri walked out of the service building and over to the aircraft. Jack opened the door and jumped down, then turned and helped Nicole.

'Papa,' she said with obvious delight, as she hugged and kissed her father.

'Nicole Elizabeth, solnishka moi, it's wonderful to have you back. You look so well.'

'You too, daddy. Olga is looking after you I think.'

A room boy helped Mike take Nicole's luggage from the cargo stowage and load it onto a small buggy.

'Good evening Miss Nicole, I'll take the luggage to your villa.'

'Thank you,' she replied with a smile.

She then turned to the pilot and said, 'Thanks, Mike.'

'My pleasure, Miss Nicole.'

'Okay let's get you up to the house,' said Dimitri.

Jack watched as the two walked off the helipad and climbed into the buggy, arms round each other's waist. Theirs was a wonderful relationship and it was clear, even with all his wealth, that Nicole was the only thing that mattered to him.

'Dad, I'd like to get a quick shower and change, then we'll come up to the house

'Okay, I'll see you in an hour for dinner.' He kissed her and got into another buggy and drove off. Jack got in beside Nicole and set off for their villa, taking the beach road, so she could see the sunset.

'It is so wonderful here,' she said, 'And being here with you, darling, is the best.'

'I've missed you, Nikki.'

They arrived at the villa as the room boy was leaving, 'Have a good evening, Miss Nicole, sir,' he said, as he walked away.

She kicked off her heels and sat on the couch, he came over to her and kissed her hard this time.

'I need a shower, darling.' she said, and stood up.

He watched her as she walked through into the main bedroom, then through into the dressing room. 'How was your flight, Nikki?'

'It was okay, darling; the service is really good on Etihad.'

He went into the bedroom and could hear the shower running. He quickly undressed and quietly walked into the big bathroom. She had her back to him, her head back and the water splashing over her body. Her back and buttocks glistened in the steamy soapy water. He stepped in and pressed hard up against her back, kissed her neck and cupped her breasts.

'What kept you?' she said.

Chapter Thirty One
'The Wild Bunch'

Tom and the guys waited in the VIP departure lounge, at Kuwait airport. They had been sent diplomatic documentation from the Russian Embassy in Abu Dhabi, via Olga, which effectively entitled them to travel as diplomats. They had bought three large suitcases from the Safwan duty free store, packed the diamonds into one and their weapons into the other two. Tom had considered sending the weapons back to Baghdad with the Landcruisers, but thought better of it.

Olga had emailed 'diplomatic bag' labels, with the relevant serial numbers and documentation, which Ian had printed out and fixed to the suitcases.

Their arrival at the airport and subsequent VIP treatment, plus the circumvention of customs, had annoyed several of the Kuwait airport officials, but there was little they could do.

'We could have anything in the bloody cases,' said Danny.

'That's right,' said Steve, 'We have a shit load of diamonds and weapons!'

'So any diplomat can bring anything they want into any country?'

Danny was about to continue blabbering on, when the lounge manager approached and said,

'Good morning. Your aircraft is ready. If you would care to follow me, please.'

The luxury shuttle bus took them to the stand and pulled up alongside the Orel Corporation executive jet; the eagle's head resplendent on the fuselage and tail.

'Ahh, now you're talking,' said Ian, 'This is a wee bit'o class.'

They picked up the three suitcases and carried them onto the small jet, along with their personal bags. The attendant helped them stow the bags in the rear of the aircraft and they all took their seats. The captain came from the cabin and said, 'Good morning lady and gentlemen. We will be taking off shortly, so please relax and enjoy the flight.'

* * *

Umm Qasr is Iraq's only seaport and has been the country's gateway to the Arabian gulf, for over three thousand years. It has always been a thriving international facility, but since the beginning of Operation Iraqi Freedom, the port was now essentially controlled by the Coalition.

That said, the vast numbers of fishing and pearl diving dhows that used the port, were not under the scrutiny of the military and were able to come and go as normal.

Jamal had 'commandeered' a large fishing dhow, The Fatimah and he and the other five ISIL insurgents were making ready to set sail. They had concealed weapons and radio equipment in the old smuggler's compartment in the bowels of the hull and covered the hatch with nets and fishing equipment. If they were stopped and searched, there was little chance they would be found to be anything other than fishermen.

'Let's get moving,' Jamal shouted.

The men at the bow and stern slipped the mooring lines. The engine belched black smoke from the exhaust and the vessel slipped out of the harbour and into the shimmering waters of the Gulf. Jamal went into the wheelhouse, looked at the map and said to the helmsman, 'About thirty-five hours sailing?'

'Yes, brother. We shall be off the coast of Abu Dhabi tomorrow evening, Inshallah.'

* * *

The Orel jet landed at Abu Dhabi and taxied to the private aviation area. Tom and the team disembarked and were shuttled across to the VIP lounge by luxury minibus. The girls in the lounge had their passports processed swiftly and the guys were back on the mini bus and across to the helipad where Dimitri's helicopter was waiting. Mike was there as they all piled off the bus. *Who the hell are this bunch,* he thought to himself, then moved forward to help with their luggage.

'Good morning, everyone,' said Mike.

'Morning, I'm Tom,' he said as he shook Mike's hand.

'There are six seats in the cabin and one up front next to me, if anyone wants to use it.'

'I'll have that one,' shouted Danny, before anyone else had an chance to reply.

Steve put his hand over his friend's mouth and said, 'Do you want to sit up front, Lisa?'

'I'd love to,' she said, as she smiled at Mike.

The guys piled into the opulent aircraft and settled into the comfortable seats. A few moments later, Mike's voice came over the speaker. 'Please check your seat belts everyone.' He then began his swift pre-flight check. 'Eagle six seven one, request clearance please.'

A few moment later a voice came back, 'Eagle six seven one, you are clear to proceed.'

'Copy that, thank you control.'

The rotors turned slowly, gained momentum and increased speed as the pilot turned the throttle to maximum. Within a few seconds they were in the air and rising above the airfield and out over the city.

'This is the life,' said Ian, as they flew over the Gulf and dropped to five hundred feet.

They had all been in helicopters at one time or another, but a military or civilian chopper was no comparison to the enjoyment, of the luxurious Eurocopter.

The pilot's voice came over the speakers, 'Orel Island dead ahead, ETA five minutes everyone.'

Tom had been to the island a couple of times with Jack, but the rest of the guys had only heard of the place. A couple of kilometres out, the aircraft banked to the left and circled the island.

'That is a beautiful place,' said Lisa.

'It's like a resort,' said Ian.

'Only Dimitri lives here?' said Danny.

'Yes,' said Tom, 'But he runs his corporation from here and there's lots of staff. He regularly has friends and business people stay as well, I believe.'

'Orel Island, this is eagle six seven one, permission to land.'

'Eagle six seven one, clear to land.'

'Roger Orel Island, thank you.'

Jack and Nicole watched the aircraft land from the service building and, as soon as the doors were open, they walked out to the helipad. Danny turned to Tom and quietly said, 'Is that Nicole?'

'Yes.'

'Wow!' said Danny.

There were four buggies lined up next to the service building and three drivers. The drivers moved to the cargo stowage and off-loaded the personal bags and then Jack saw the three suitcases. 'Three bags full?' he said to Tom.

'I didn't want to send the weapons back with the vehicles, they could have ended up anywhere,' said Tom, quietly.

'Quite right,' said Jack, as he put his arm round Tom's shoulder, 'Good to see you all.'

'Everyone, this is Nicole. It's getting a bit warm, so we'll go up to the mansion and do introductions there.'

Nicole went over to Tom and kissed his cheek, 'Lovely to see you again, Tom.'

'You too, Nicole, looking fabulous as ever,' he said with a wink.

'Are you keeping my guy safe?'

'Always.'

She kissed his cheek and then went over to Lisa, 'Hello, I'm Nicole, you're Lisa.'

'Yes, it's lovely to meet you, Nicole, and great to be here, in such a wonderful place.'

'You're very welcome, come on, ride with us to the house.'

Chapter Thirty Two
'Lunch on the Veranda'

Dimitri was at the big desk, telephone in hand, when Nicole entered the study.

'Papa!'

'Solnishka, how are you my darling?'

They hugged and kissed for a few moments, then he said, 'And these are our guests?'

'Yes. But we haven't done introductions yet.'

Tom walked over and offered Dimitri his hand, 'Good to see you again, sir.'

As he shook his hand, he said, 'Tom, pleased to have you here again and I've told you before, call me Mitri.'

'Yes, sir, Mitri.'

'So who have we here, Jack?' he said, as he offered Lisa his hand.

'This is, Lisa,'

'Pleasure to meet you, sir,' she said, as he kissed her hand.

'Mitri, please, call me Mitri, we're all friends here. You are American? New York?'

'Yes, but I work in DC, for the Washington Post.'

'Right, then I'd better watch what I say,' he said with a laugh.

Jack introduced each of the team to Dimitri and Nicole, after which, Dimitri said, 'Okay guys, if you want to get cleaned up, we can all meet for lunch in an hour.'

'Jack, the bags?' said Tom.

'Take two to your bungalow; leave the one with the stones in here. That's okay, Mitri?'

'Of course,' he said, 'It will be quite safe here.'

'When am I going to find out what this is all about,' said Nicole, 'Jack has told me nothing.'

'All will be revealed over lunch,' said Jack.

A buffet lunch had been laid out on the huge veranda. A bar had been set up at the side and when Jack and Nicole arrived, Lisa, Tom and Santosh were already there, with Dimitri.

'Hi guys,' said Jack, 'where's the rest of the boys?'

'We're here,' said Ian, 'I had to go and get these two off the jet skis.'

'Bloody tourists,' said Tom, and everyone laughed.

'Please. Everyone, help yourselves to food and drink,' said Dimitri, 'I thought it better we don't have any staff here while we talk.' As he finished speaking Olga arrived, 'Except, Olga of course.'

Tom went over to Olga and said, 'Hello, Olga, great to see you again.'

'You, too, Tom,' she said with a gleaming smile.

Tom introduced the rest of the group to Olga in turn, Danny clearly smitten.

With a chuckle, Lisa said to, Tom. 'Looks like I'm off Danny's radar.'

'Mmm,' smiled Tom. 'How fickle is the Geordie heart,' they both laughed.

Dimitri said, 'Everyone. Please, let's eat,' then, as he walked to the table, turned to Steve and pointed to the eye patch. 'I hope you didn't lose that on the mission, Steve?'

'No, sir, I lost this in the Falklands, saving Danny's ass.'

'I hope it was worth it?' said Dimitri, with a grin.

'I wonder sometimes,' said Steve, also with a grin.

'I heard that,' said Danny, 'Thanks a lot.'

Steve outstretched his arm in Danny's direction, flat palm open. Danny walked over and slapped it, as he whispered, 'Bastard!' then winked at Steve.

When they were settled, Jack began the whole story, as Nicole listened, fascinated.

When he had finished, she said, 'So the big case in Dad's study is full of diamonds?'

'Yeah,' said Jack.

'Can I see them?'

They took their drinks back into the house and went to Dimitri's study. Tom nodded to Santosh, who pulled the case to the big coffee table, in the middle of the sitting area. Ian helped him lift the heavy case onto the low table and unzipped it. They opened the bag and inside were two smaller cloth drawstring bags. Ian lifted out one and Santosh lifted out the other. Ian opened his, revealing the uncut stones. 'Oh my God, that's all uncut diamonds?' said Nicole.

'Yeah,' said Jack, 'Wait till you see this.' He nodded to Ian, who opened his bag revealing the discoloured packets. Ian picked out two packets and passed one to Nicole and one to Dimitri.

They opened the packets and poured the tiny bundles of sparkling diamonds onto the table. Nicole looked at her father and then turned to Jack and said, 'You *have,* been bad boys.'

'On the contrary,' said Dimitri, 'How many did you say you have Jack?'

'Tom, you got the weights?'

Tom took out his wallet and removed a small piece of paper, handing it to Dimitri, said   'We used a kitchen scales to weigh them, so it's not going to be exact, but near enough.'

'Kitchen scales?' said Dimitri, as he let out a laugh, 'That's priceless.'

'Not priceless, Mitri,' said Danny, 'Santosh paid a hundred bucks for those scales.' This time everyone laughed.

'Okay, you have over forty kilos of cut and uncut stones, and you estimate value at about one and a quarter billion,' said Dimitri.

'*How much?*' said Nicole.

'Yes, we think one point two billion, plus,' said Tom.

'My gemmologists will be here later today. They will appraise both lots and give us an accurate count. Probably take a couple of days for them to complete the task. In the meantime, Olga, will you look at the latest diamond price, cut and uncut please. Then we have an idea of how accurate your original estimate is.'

'Yes, sir, it shouldn't take me too long.'

He handed her the slip of paper with the weights and she left the study.

'We now need to discuss what we are going to do with these,' he said, waving his hand over the bags of diamonds. 'Everyone get drinks and let's make ourselves comfortable in here.'

'Yes,' said Jack, 'Dimitri and I discussed disposal yesterday. And if you all agree, he will arrange everything for us.'

'Okay,' said Tom. 'So what's the plan?'

'First we get an accurate count, which will take a couple of days. So you guys will have to rough it here for a day, or two.'

Everyone laughed as Ian said, 'Och, is there nae a decent hotel round here?'

'Dimitri will take the diamonds from us, for eighty percent of their wholesale value.'

'Sounds good to me,' said Tom, 'Considering we were happy to take twenty percent reward, from the bloody Kuwaitis.'

'Exactly,' continued Jack

'Really,' said Dimitri, a stern look on his face, 'I've been conned.'

Everyone looked at him and then he burst out laughing, 'Carry on, Jack.'

'The uncut stones, which we believe are conflict diamonds, we will give to Dimitri.'

'That's quite a big slice, isn't it, Jack?' said Tom, 'No offence intended, Mitri.'

'None taken, Tom, but let Jack continue.'

'As I said, we give the conflict stones to Dimitri and he will arrange to have them cut and polished; which will increase their value tenfold. He will then give the wholesale value of the newly cut stones, to various charities of our choice. That way, there'll be some good comes from them. We will also get Ali Wassam's family out to Turkey and give them a million.'

'Sounds an excellent plan,' said Lisa.

'I agree,' said Ian.

'Okay by me,' said Danny.

'Me too,' said Steve

'Okay with me, boss,' said Santosh.

'Tom. Okay with you?' said Jack.

'Perfect. Just perfect.'

'What about our shares, boss? I canny stick forty odd million in the Royal Bank of Scotland,' said Ian.

'Mitri will arrange numbered offshore accounts for us all.'

Dimitri stood and said, 'Yes, gentlemen,' then nodded to Lisa, 'And lady. I suggest you all consider a minimum of three accounts, spread the money about, not good all in one place. We can set them up for you in Switzerland, the Caymans, Andorra, or Hong Kong perhaps. I'll have Olga arrange them for you, in the next couple of days. Soon as we have the final value, I will have my bank make the transfer of your shares, to each of your accounts, as per your instructions.'

'So, we really are going to be millionaires?' said Danny.

'That's right,' said Dimitri, 'Just don't spend it all at once.'

Again everyone laughed, when Danny said, 'Just don't tell my wife!'

Chapter Thirty Three
'Proposal'

After lunch, the guys went back to their accommodation, to relax or enjoy the time on Orel Island. Nicole and Jack stayed with Dimitri, 'So, Dad, what you been up to?' she said, 'You are looking very well, darling.'

'Yes I'm fine, Nicole, not as good as I would like to be, but still capable.'

'Yes, but capable of what?' she said, 'Olga is looking after you?'

Dimitri just smiled and continued, 'I got back from Japan a couple of days ago. We bought a shipyard and we are going to build oil-tankers. But what about you? How was the new spa opening? Did you get the footballers' wives?'

'Yes, it was terrific. It's a great location in the city and yes, we had a lot of your footie friends' wives.'

She turned to Jack, 'And, you, Jack Castle, what have you been up to?'

'What?' he said smiling.

'A million to Ali Wassam's family. What did that mean, Zaikin? There's something you're not telling me?'

She knew he had a dangerous job and she knew he enjoyed the work and camaraderie. But she had wanted him to give it up, even before he set up the company for the Baghdad contracts. She knew he always played down any incidents, to limit her worry and concern.

'We had a bit of trouble at the oasis. We were attacked and Ali was killed.'

She stood up and put her arms around him, 'I didn't know, Ali. God bless him. This money will let you do something else, Zaikin. I don't want you to go back to Iraq.'

The knock on the door broke the tension in the study and Olga walked in. She handed Dimitri a smart folder and said, 'Excuse me, sir, here's the latest prices for cut and uncut, plus the values for the amounts you gave me.'

'Thank you, Olga,' he said, opening the folder.

'Will there be anything else, sir?'

'Yes. We need to set up numbered accounts for Jack and his guys. If you could talk to each of them, see where they prefer to have them, please.'

'Very good sir, I'll get on it right away.'

'Thank you, Olga,' he said, with a smile.

'You're welcome, sir,' returning his smile. 'Is there anything you need, Nicole?'

'No, everything's lovely in the villa, thank you, Olga. But I want to have a catch up with you, as soon as you have time. And I still want you to come over to London. When dad gives you some time off.'

'Yes, we need some girl time,' said Olga, then turning to her boss said, 'Excuse me, sir.'

'Okay you two, off you go, have some fun,' said Dimitri.

After they had left, he went out onto the veranda and saw Lisa sitting in the shade.

'What's this, all alone young lady?'

Lisa stood up and smiled, 'Yes, it's just so beautiful here. I thought I'd enjoy it, now the boys have all gone. I can go back to my bungalow if I'm disturbing you, sir.'

'You're not disturbing me and please, you must call me, Mitri. May I join you?'

She gave a slight laugh, 'It's your house, you can do what you like. But sure, I'd love to chat with you, Mitri.'

He went over to the bar and took a small bottle of expensive mineral water from the fridge, 'Would you like something, Lisa? Champagne, wine? I make a mean cocktail.'

'A cold beer would be lovely, please.'

Jack and Nicole were walking along the beach and Dimitri waved. He sat down and said, 'Now then, tell me all about yourself?'

'Actually, sir, Mitri, I was hoping to hear about you.'

'Oh my life is an open book, Lisa, you just need to Google me. I think they have me in as one of the world's top fifty wealthiest men.' They both laughed.

'I was more interested in the real *you* and how you met Nicole's mother?'

'Ah, yes, me. Am I talking to a journalist, or a friend?'

'Most definitely a friend, Mitri,' she said with a smile.

'Very well,' He took a sip of the water and said, 'I met Elizabeth in London, in 1970. I was there on business, but one of my people had committed me to a summer ball, for a children's charity. Elizabeth was on the organising committee for the charity and I was introduced to her when I arrived. She was a stunningly beautiful woman.'

His eyes glazed over and Lisa looked away, took a sip of her beer, and gave the old man a few moments with his memories.

'Yes, she was a beautiful woman, in every sense of the word,' he said as he cleared his throat.

'So, I had a couple of dances with her and I was overwhelmed; truly love at first sight.'

'Romantic!'

'Yes indeed and the same for her. But I didn't know that 'til some time later,' he continued, with a smile.

'So, before I left, I asked her to lunch the next day. She agreed and we met at Claridges. She was quite scathing about eating at such an extravagant place, but she, *we,* enjoyed a wonderful afternoon together.'

'Sounds lovely.'

'The next morning, I sent her a very nice watch, with a note of thanks and an invitation to dinner. We met a couple of days later and I took her to a little Italian in Soho, she loved that. I noticed she wasn't wearing the watch.'

'Oh?'

'I asked if she didn't like it, because her note had said it was lovely. She put her hand on mine and said, '*Yes, it was beautiful and I got ten thousand pounds for it, which I have donated on your behalf, to the children's charity.*'

'Oh no!' laughed Lisa.

Dimitri smiled as well and continued, 'I never told her I paid fifteen thousand for it!'

'So, what happened next?'

'Well, we had another wonderful evening and I dropped her back at her flat. The following day, I went to an animal rescue place. I gave them a donation and chose the most beaten-up cat they had. He was all shaved, obviously been maltreated and had scars on his head and back. He was a nervous little thing. I took him round to her flat and she burst into tears, when she saw him. She took him from me and put him on the couch, then turned and kissed me. That was it. We were married three months later, in Rome.

'Wonderful. And the cat?'

'He grew his fur and turned out to a beautiful Persian; we had him for almost ten years. Elizabeth named him Raggy, because of how he first looked.'

'What a lovely story.'

Olga arrived and said, 'Excuse me, sir; there's an urgent call for you, from St Petersburg.'

'Thank you, Olga.'

'Please excuse me, Lisa, I hope I didn't bore you with my story?'

'It was lovely, Mitri. See you later.'

* * *

The Fatimah had made good progress down the length of the Arabian Gulf. Jamal had gone over and over the plan with his five accomplices and was happy he would succeed in his mission and win the favour and respect of his father.

'My brothers of the sword, The Islamic State of Iraq and the Levant will know our names and call us heros, for what we are about to do. And should we die, Inshallah, we shall be called hero and martyr.'

Then, with raised fists, they all screamed, 'Allah o Akbah, Allah o Akbah, Allah o Akbah.'

* * *

The two villas and six bungalows, all had their own section of beach, each with a couple of canopied four poster sunbeds on a raised wooden deck. Electricity had been run out to the beach and there was lighting and cooling fans under each canopy. A refrigerator, filled with water, soft drinks, beers, wine and champagne, made it the ultimate in sunbathing.

'Maybe we should just take up this life all the time, Zaikin?'

'But wouldn't we get bored, darling?'

'I guess we would, but I really want you to consider a change of career now, old man.'

'Old man?'

'Well, you're not fifty any more, darling.' she said, with a cheeky grin.

'Come back inside and I'll show you what an ol' man can do.'

She jumped up with a squeal and ran into the sea. Jack watched her run down the beach. The tiny bikini didn't cover a much of her bottom, '*Yum, yum,* he thought. Then ran after her.

It was late afternoon when the shuttle boat arrived with the two Indian gemmologists. Tom was swimming with Lisa and saw the boat arrive at the small marina along the beach.

'I guess these are Mitri's diamond guys,' said Tom.

Lisa looked over towards the boat as it tied up at the dock. 'Yes, we'll soon know just how much we are talking about, I still can't believe it.'

'I'll believe it when there are three bank accounts, stuffed with money,' he said.

She laughed and in a Southern drawl said, 'Oh, yes, siree. It 'aint over, 'til that fat lady sings.'

Dinner was arranged for eight o clock at the mansion. Normally Dimitri and any island guests would dress for dinner, but on this occasion the protocol had been waived, due to the lack of appropriate attire by Jack's boys.

Everyone gathered for drinks at seven thirty on the veranda. The mood was relaxed but excited as the magnitude of their good fortune had begun to sink in.

'I will build a house in England and move my family there,' said Santosh.

'Not more bloody immigrants!' said Danny. 'At least you won't need to claim benefit.'

Santosh laughed and said, 'No, and you'll be able *to stop* claiming.'

Again they both laughed and slapped a high five.

'What about you, Ian?' said Steve, 'What's your plan?'

'Ah'm nae sure really. Maybe a world cruise, to think about it.'

'How about you, Jack?' said Tom, 'What you going to do?'

'I think I might get married.'

'Oh yes and who are you planning to marry?' said Nicole, a look of feigned concern on her face.

'Ah, right, yes,' said Jack, 'Nicole Elizabeth Orlov, will you marry me?'

She gave him a disapproving look and then flashed a beautiful smile, her eyes moist. She hugged and kissed him, then stood back and said, 'Of course, darling. But where's the ring?'

'Hold on a wee minute,' said Ian, 'I'll just pop in the house and see if I cannae find a spare diamond.'

Everyone laughed, Dimitri embraced his daughter, 'I'm so happy for you my darling,' then shook Jack's hand, 'It's about time my boy.'

'I know. But now I might just be able to keep her, in the manner she's accustomed to.'

'Okay, everyone, let's go eat and celebrate,' said Dimitri.

The evening meal was excellent, wine and champagne flowed, but Tom had warned the guys to behave. 'Have a drink,' he had told them, 'But behave yourselves, while you're on the island.'

And for the most part they had; there were still the ribald comments, albeit toned down a lot, but the constant 'piss taking' between them, never stopped.

It was almost midnight when the party broke up and everyone returned to their respective villas and bungalows. The crescent moon hung low in the sky and the stars sparkled over Orel Island. As they walked along the beach, he turned to her and said, 'This is a beautiful place Nikki, and you are beautiful.'

She put her arm round his waist, her head against his shoulder, 'I love you Jack, I'm so happy.'

'I love you too darling. Time for bed I think.'

Chapter Thirty Four
'Kidnapped'

The rusty anchor rattled over the side of the Fatimah and hit the water with a noisy splash. Jamal looked at his watch and said, 'It's after midnight, brothers, get the inflatable ready. I want to be on the island in an hour.'

The night sky was clear and a mild northerly breeze blew down the Gulf. The light inflatable boat, with its hundred and twenty horsepower engine, skipped across the waves effortlessly. Jamal and his two accomplices were low down in the bottom of the boat, their heads just above the fat inflated rim of the craft. The island was dead ahead and they slowed the engine to an almost crawl, then cut it and allowed the boat to wash in silently; with the small waves breaking on the beach. Adil Mubarak, had told them everything they needed to know about Jack Castle, his woman and the island, as well as the villa they always used. He had even provided photographs of Castle and the woman. He had been very cooperative, thought Jamal.

There were all-night pathway lights, around the island and every flower bed and tree was illuminated, but the rest of the property was in relative darkness. The beach was in shadow, from the water's edge, right up to the villa. Mubarak had told them of the infra-red security cameras and security men, so they had to move fast and as soon as the boat touched the beach, Jamal and one of the men leapt out and sprinted at top speed to the villa.

The patio doors were closed, but foolishly, not locked. The two insurgents entered silently and moved swiftly across the floor to the bedroom. As they approached the bed, Jack woke and shouted, 'Nicole!'

The two dark figures closed in on him and the last thing he felt, before losing consciousness, was the searing pain at the side of his head.

He had only been out for a few seconds and his head was causing him a lot of pain, but he was on his feet and running naked down the beach, towards Nicole's muted screams. He could see the two men bundling her naked body into the boat, a third man at the stern, the big powerful outboard running. They would be away in seconds. She was in the bottom of the boat now, her legs kicking at the air, in an effort to stop them holding her down.

In his peripheral vision, Jack saw two security men running along the beach, their weapons drawn. 'Don't shoot!' he yelled.

He did not want Nicole shot in a firefight. Jack used all the power left in his legs, to cover the last few metres between him and the kidnappers. He could hear the security men shouting behind him, as he pushed off with all his remaining strength and dived at the man controlling the motor. The man tried to sidestep Jack, but in the tiny craft there was nowhere to move and he was caught on the shoulder. The force of Jack's leap, took both of them over the side and into the waves. He was under water and the younger, fitter man was getting the better of him. Holding his breath, Jack reacted and kneed the man hard in the testicles. Then, out of the water and after a huge gulp of air, Jack grabbed the man by the front of his shirt, pulled him close and head butted him, full in the face. The man fell back onto the wet sand. Jack quickly turned, only to see the boat disappearing into the darkness of the Gulf.

The security men were with him now and had the stunned and bleeding kidnapper in their grasp. The shouting had woken the guys and Tom and Lisa came running down the beach followed by the rest of the team.

'What the fuck's going on?' said Tom.

'They've kidnapped, Nicole!' said Jack, as he tried to steady his breath.

'Who have?' said Lisa.

'I don't know, but this, bastard does. And we're gonna find out, right now.'

They took the kidnapper up to the mansion and tied him into a chair on the terrace.

Dimitri had dressed and was with the group. He looked at the bloodied and bleeding, kidnapper.

'Tell me where my daughter is and you may still live.'

The man looked at Dimitri and the infidels surrounding him, then spoke proudly in Arabic.

'What's he saying?' said Dimitri.

'He said he'll tell you nothing and that he's not afraid,' said Santosh.

Dimitri took Jack aside, 'You know Nicole has a micro-tracer in her thigh, don't you Jack.'

'Yes of course, it's been there for years, since you had that kidnap threat from the Chechens, but we need to know what we are up against, now, before we go after her, Mitri.'

'I understand, Jack. Do what you have to do.'

'Lisa, go in the house. You don't need to see this,' said Jack, 'Steve, go get something from the kitchen, to make this fucker talk.'

'Hang on, Steve,' said Tom.

The man was young and strong and had taken the initial beating bravely. It was clear to Jack that he was a fanatic and pain was not something that would make him talk.

'We are running out of time, Tom,' said Jack.

'I know,' said Tom, 'Steve, Danny, go see if you can find a chef's blow-torch in the kitchen.'

'Gotcha,' said Steve, as he turned to go in the house.

'Just a minute,' shouted Tom, 'I need a few more things as well.'

Danny and Steve found the huge kitchen and Danny said, 'F'fucks sake, look at the size of this place, it's like a bloody hotel.'

'Shut it, Dan, just find the stuff.'

When they returned to the veranda, they saw the kidnapper's clothes had been cut from him and he now sat naked, arms and legs still tied to the chair. The blood had been wiped from his face and mouth and a blindfold had been tied around his eyes.

'Here's the stuff you wanted, Tom,'

Jack looked at the items Tom had asked for and nodded, 'Good thinking, Tom. It might work.'

The kidnapper did not understand what was happening, but he trembled each time he felt them touch his body. He heard the noise of something being unwrapped and applied to his arms, legs and chest. The smell was unfamiliar, he could not place it. His imagination caused the fear to manifest and he began to shake uncontrollably.

'What the hell is this all about?' whispered Danny.

'Shut up and watch,' said Steve

'Pass me the blow-torch,' said Tom.

Ian picked up the torch and handed it to Tom. Santosh looked on, unsure what was about to happen.

'Take the blindfold off.'

Santosh moved to the man and slowly removed the cloth from around the man's face. The kidnapper blinked a few times, then looked down at his body and arms. He began to jabber in Arabic. He pulled at his restraints and tried to shake the foul items from his body. His arms chest and legs had been covered with strips of bacon and secured in place with cling-film. He looked ridiculous, but the unclean meat, held firm in place on his body, had repulsed him and he tried to escape from the bindings.

Tom fired up the blow torch and the man's eyes widened, in the young face.

'Santosh, translate, word for word.'

'Yes, boss.'

Tom stood close to the trembling kidnapper and spoke slowly, 'What is your name?'

'Farad, I am, Farad.'

'Okay, Farad, I am sure before you embarked on this mission, you prepared your body for possible death. You prayed and cleansed your body. Yes?'

'Yes, I was cleansed.'

The kidnapper flinched, as Tom gently touched the cling film, 'You know what this is?'

The man nodded and said, 'Yes, it is swine, unclean pork. Swine.'

'Okay good, Farad, you understand. I am going to burn this unclean swine into your flesh.   You will not be able to cleanse your body. The swine will be part of your body. You will become swine, do you understand.'

The man's eyes were wide and his voice trembled, he was uttering prayers as Tom continued, his voice calm and soft.

'If you die as swine, you will never be able to enter heaven. You will not enter as a martyr. You will not go to the highest place in heaven, the place reserved for prophets and martyrs. You will not even be allowed into the first level of heaven. Your eternal spirit will exist in the hell of infidels and the unclean heathen. Do you understand Farad?'

The kidnapper was shaking now, tears fell from his eyes and the fear for his soul overcame his bodily functions, as piss ran down his legs. Tom stood back, as the urine pooled between the man's bare feet.

'Pass me his T-shirt.'

Tom put down the blow-torch, knelt down and mopped up the urine, as the man watched. Then stood in front of the kidnapper and wrung out the shirt over the man's head. Farad shook his head to rid himself of the fluid, but it soaked through his hair and down his face.

'You are truly unclean now, Farad, and you will die as filth and never enter heaven.'

Tom picked up the blow-torch, ignited it again and moved slowly, menacingly, towards the trembling man.

'No. No. No' screamed the kidnapper, 'I will tell you anything you wish to know.'

Tom switched of the torch, turned to Jack and said, 'All yours, Jack, I think he wants to have a chat now.'

'Don't suppose there's any chance of a bacon sandwich?' said Danny.

The kidnapper had told them everything he knew, but Jack could not understand how they had found out so much, about him and where to find him.

He turned to Tom and said, 'These bastards have had good intel, but from where?'

'The only people who knew you would be here were our guys and Dimitri,' said Tom.

'No. I told Adil Mubarak, I'd be here with Nikki.'

Jack took out his cell phone and pressed his partner's number. The phone rang for several seconds; then a voice he did not recognise said, 'Hello?'

'Adil? Is that you? This is Jack.'

'Hello, Mr Castle, this is Karim, his son.'

'Oh, hello again, Karim, I'm sorry to disturb you at this time of night, but something terrible has happened and I need to speak with your father urgently.'

'I'm sorry, Mr Castle, but something terrible has happened here as well.'

The line went silent for a several seconds, then Jack said, 'Karim?'

'Yes, I'm here, sir,' then in a quiet, trembling voice, said, 'My father and mother have been murdered.'

Chapter Thirty Five
'Rescue'

They were all in the study. Mike was on the phone to Gary, Dimitri's other pilot. 'We need your helicopter here on the island immediately. No. Just make sure it's fully fuelled. Yes. Yes. See you soon,' he hung up, then stood and continued listening to the rest of the rescue plan.

'You sure these Sea Doo's are powerful enough for us, Mitri?' said Tom.

'Yes, they are good at full power, for about thirty minutes.'

'That's plenty,' said Steve, 'I've used them before.'

'What are they exactly?' said Santosh quietly to Danny.

'They're like a small torpedo, with a powerful battery operated motor, they pull you through the water, on the surface or below,' whispered Danny.

'Ah yeah, I know. I have seen these in the dive shop.'

Dimitri, Jack and Ian, were at the big desk watching the tiny signal, on the special tracking equipment.

'This is a great piece of kit,' said Ian, 'It shows where she is, down to the last square metre.'

Olga came in and said, 'Wet suits are ready for you and your men, at the helipad.'

'Thanks, Olga,' said Tom, 'Danny, Steve, go bring the bags down to the helipad and check over the weapons.'

'Take the receiver with you,' said Dimitri.

'Ian, pick that up and make sure you know where she is at all times.'

'Din'ae worry, boss, we won't lose her.'

The phone rang and Mike picked it up, 'Okay, thanks.'

'Gary's here with the second helicopter, he's landing now.'

'Good, thanks, Mike,' said Jack, 'Okay, let's move.' He turned to Dimitri and they hugged. 'Jack, please bring my daughter back.'

'I will, Mitri, I will.'

The tiny convoy of buggies rolled up to the service building. Inside, Danny and Steve had the cases open and the weapons spread out on the expensive leather couch.

They checked over the wet suits and, with help from the pilots, Tom, Danny and Steve, struggled into them. Ian handed Santosh his MP5, then picked up his own, both efficiently checked and loaded the weapons. Jack took his Glock, checked the breach, loaded it and slipped the weapon inside his shirt.

The three Sea Doos were sitting on the floor, their high gloss finish and gleaming chrome work gave the impression of a day out on the boat.

'These look cool,' said Steve. 'I've never seen any as big as these. Good old, Dimitri.'

Mike quickly briefed Gary on the intended mission and agreed call signs.

'Gary's aircraft will be Eagle Two. Mine, Eagle One,' he said to Jack.

'Okay thanks Mike. Everyone got the call signs?'

'Yes, boss,' from Santosh, Danny and Steve.

'Got it,' said Ian and Tom.

'Okay, guys,' said Tom. 'Let's mount up.'

Back on the veranda, Dimitri, Olga and Lisa, watched in silence, as the two helicopters lifted off and vanished into the dark night. Olga turned to her boss and put her arms round him, then whispered something into his ear. Lisa could not hear what she had said, but did notice the tears in the tough old Russian's eyes.

Ian was in the seat next to Mike, so the pilot could follow the directions on the scanner.

Jack said into the headset, 'Ian, how we doing buddy?'

'Signal is very strong and constant, nae problems at all.'

'How far away buddy?'

'Looks tae be twenty-two kliks and moving directly north.'

'How long to her location?'

'Not long,' said Mike, 'ETA approximately twelve minutes.'

Mike's voice came over the headsets in both aircraft, 'ETA, twelve minutes, stand by.'

The guys in Eagle Two checked the waterproof covers on their side arms and made a final check of the Sea Doos.

'You two okay?' said Tom.

'Good,' said Danny and gave a thumbs-up.

Steve removed his eye patch and put it in the zip-pocket of the wet suit, 'I'm good, Tom.'

Chapter Thirty Six
'End Game'

Eagle Two approached from the south, with the navigation lights off, the darkness shielded it from anyone at the stern of the dhow. It slowed to almost stall speed and hovered just above the water, then Gary shouted, 'Good to go?'

'Good to go,' shouted Tom, as he slid open the side door of the aircraft.

The wake from the dhow, at this distance had dissipated and it made it easier for Tom, Steve and Danny to drop into the water, with their equipment. The three splashed into the waves and the helicopter moved to the side, to reduce the downdraft, while the pilot waited until he had a thumbs-up from each of the men. He saw they all had their Sea Doos powered up and had assumed a three abreast formation, as they increased speed towards the dhow ahead.

* * *

Eagle One circled the vessel, causing three men to appear on deck.

Jack tried to raise the dhow on the short-wave, but after several unsuccessful attempts, Mike said, 'Try the loudspeaker,' then flipped a switch on the control panel, nodded at Jack and said, 'Go ahead.'

'This is the UAE Gulf Patrol, please cut your engines; we wish to inspect your vessel.'

'Maybe they din'ae understand English,' said Ian.

'Well, unless they understand English or Russian we gotta problem, coz I don't speak fucking Arabic.'

'Mike, can you come around in front of them, put your spotlight on the deck?'

'Stand by.'

'Fishing dhow Fatimah, cut your engines and prepare to be boarded.

The three men on deck watched, as the helicopter moved to the front of the ship and hovered.

'Jamal, we cannot be boarded,' said one of the three.

Jamal turned to his subordinate and in a calm voice said, 'Be calm, brother, go and get your weapons.'

'Fuck this,' said Ian, as he slid the side door open. He raised his MP5 to his shoulder and said, 'Hold it a wee bit steady, Mike,' then fired a short burst at the navigation light, atop the mast.

Broken glass and shattered wood, rained down on the two men, which prompted them to run to the side of the ship and wave frantically. The dhow began to slow down and Jack said, 'Well done, buddy.'

'They must have a man below, with, Nicole,' said Jack.

'Why?' said Ian.

'Three on deck, one in the wheel house, last man with, Nikki.'

'Could be two in the wheel house,' said Ian.

'If I were in charge down there, I'd have a man with the hostage,' said Jack. 'Okay, run the winch out, Mike. I'm going down.'

'Let's hope the boys have caught up and can get on board,' said Ian.

'Yeah, let's hope so! Keep me covered buddy.'

'Nae bother, big man.'

* * *

The Sea Doos were every bit as good as Dimitri had said and they pulled the three men through the water swiftly and in relative quiet. Tom said, 'The dhow's stopped engines. It's slowing down!'

They kept up the pace and a few minutes later, were about thirty metres from the stern. Tom made a cut throat gesture with his hand and they all cut the motors on the Sea Doos, then began swimming towards the overhang at the stern of the vessel. The windows in the rear cabin were open, so they were cautious not to make any sound. Tom pointed to himself and then the window. Danny and Steve gave thumbs-up and the three began the climb up the ornate woodwork, which decorated the back of the ship.

* * *

Jack's feet touched the rolling deck and he swiftly unhooked the harness. He noticed only two men on deck now, *Where was the other? Gone for weapons,* he thought.

He knew Ian had him covered from Eagle One and then heard Eagle Two, approach from the rear. Tom, Steve and Danny should be on-board or about to be and he felt a little less exposed.

'We need to search your vessel,' he shouted, just as the third man returned with two AKs.

'Wait a minute, we are the UAE Gulf Patrol; we have a legal right to board your vessel and search. There is no need for weapons.'

The man with the AKs handed one to the guy next to him and they both turned their weapons on Jack. The third man took out a small automatic and shouted, 'Let me see your identification.'

Eagle Two now came into view and hovered close to starboard, the side door open and Santosh clearly visible; his MP5 pointed at the three men on deck.

* * *

Steve and Danny had reached the top of the dhow's stern and as they looked over the rail, could see Jack and the three insurgents. The spotlight from Eagle One blinded the three men to some extent and they held their hands to shield their eyes, from the million candle-light beam. Eagle Two had switched on its spotlight and illuminated the three men from the side. Jack had been in shadow since his feet had touched the deck, but suddenly the ship swung on the current and the beam from Eagle Two, illuminated him for several seconds. Jamal recognised him from the photographs Adil Mubarak had so helpfully provided and smiled to himself.

'We are Iraqi fisherman, returning to Umm Qasr. What reason do you have to come on board,' he shouted, continuing the charade.

'Jamal, we cannot let these infidels search the ship. Just kill him,' said the man closest.

'We are not allowing anything, brothers. Amid, take the helicopter in front. Kamal, the one to starboard. When I give the word, shoot them out of the sky. These are the men who killed, Salim and our brothers, in Iraq.'

Jack held his hands in the air and shouted, 'This can be very simple, I just need to have a look around your vessel and if there is nothing, then you will be on your way very soon.'

'Do you think we are stupid, Jack Castle, we know who you are,' shouted Jamal.

Tom looked through the cabin window and saw Nicole on the filthy bed. She was wearing a dirty white coverall, with blood down the front. Her hands and feet were bound and she had a strip of tape across her mouth. In the dim light he could see a large bruise, on her left cheek.

The young man at the door held a 9mil automatic; his ear to the door, in a futile attempt to hear the shouting on deck. A couple of low wattage bulbs provided a small amount of light, but most of the cabin was in semi darkness. The air in the cabin was pungent from stale fish, tobacco and sweat. In the corner were several boxes of television sets and another pile of boxes with cheap brand laptops; probably the owner of the vessel's smuggled stock.

Tom had two options, shoot the man now, or climb in and kill him silently. He knew if he shot him now, it would initiate the gunfight on deck and Jack would be at risk, but Steve and Danny should be in position and would cover Jack. His priority was securing Nicole, so he banked on the noise from the hovering choppers to cover his gunfire. He removed his sidearm from the waterproof bag, checked it to ensure it had not succumbed to any water ingress and snapped a round into the chamber.

* * *

Danny and Steve had slipped over the stern rail and were in cover behind the wheel house.

Through the dirty window they could see the helmsman was holding an AK47. Steve made a cut throat gesture and took the diver's knife from his belt. Danny nodded and stepped back to allow him access through the open door, his sidearm trained on the helmsman. Steve's bare feet and the noise of the helicopters made his entrance silent, as he swiftly covered the two metres to the man. Steve kicked the weapon from his grasp, grabbed him by the head, hand across his mouth. The insurgent struggled to free himself, eyes bulging, desperate for breath. With a single action Steve raised the knife and pushed it deep into the helmsman's throat.

* * *

On deck, the three men had spread out, Jamal in the centre, his side arm pointing at Jack, his subordinates weapons trained on the helicopters.

'You are making a big mistake, by taking this stance,' shouted Jack.

'You are the one making the mistake, infidel, get off the ship. Over the side. Now.'

The sound of two gun shots made Jamal look to the rear of the dhow, then swiftly turning back, saw Jack dive for cover behind a pile of rope. Jamal fired directly at the moving target, the two henchmen opened up on the helicopters. Ian and Santosh immediately returned fire.

Eagle Two was hit and began to slowly spiral and fall to the waves. Steve and Danny fired at Jamal, in an effort to keep him from shooting at Jack. Ian, in Eagle One, shot one of the insurgents, a dozen rounds thumping into his chest, knocking him over the side. Jamal had gone for cover behind a deck hatch and was returning fire to Steve and Danny, the other insurgent continued to fire on Eagle One. Not wanting to go the same way as Gary, Mike backed the aircraft away, to a reasonable safe distance.

'What the fuck you doing, Mike?' shouted Ian, 'Get me in there.'

'No good us going down as well,' shouted the pilot.

Jamal had reached across and recovered the first insurgent's AK and was now putting serious fire down on Steve and Danny. The wheel house disintegrated, as the rounds chewed the old wooden structure to pieces. The second insurgent turned his attention, from the now out of range chopper, to the two men at the rear of the dhow. The deck had become dark without the chopper spotlights and Jamal and his cohort were in shadow. Danny could make out the second shooter's outline, illuminated by the muzzle flashes from his AK. He stood up, used both hands to steady his aim and fired several shots at the muzzle flashes. The AK stopped firing and the kidnapper fell backwards, through a glass skylight, to the cabin below. Jamal had crawled along the deck and was now on the other side of the pile of ropes. 'Are you still alive, infidel,'

'Fuck you, arsehole.' shouted Jack.

'Your wife is dead now, infidel, there is nothing left for you.'

Jamal eased his way around the pile of rope and saw Jack, his back to the pile and blood seeping from a wound in his stomach. He pointed the AK at Jack's head and snarled, 'Get up, infidel.'

He pulled Jack to his feet and held the muzzle against the side of Jack's head.

'Come out,' he shouted to Danny and Steve.

'Fuck this, just shoot the bastard,' said Danny.

'He could kill the, boss, let's go,' said Steve calmly.

They left the cover of the shot-up wheelhouse and moved towards Jamal and Jack.

'Throw you weapons over the side,' said Jamal, with a snarl.

They did as he said and were quickly considering options, when Jamal turned his AK towards them. Jack was almost doubled over with pain from the stomach wound, but with all the strength he could muster, he grabbed the muzzle of the AK. The man was younger and fitter, so Jack knew he only had a second or two, before his strength would be gone. Steve and Danny ran towards the struggling couple, but Jamal had knocked Jack to the deck and turned the weapon on him.

'Down! Now!' came a shout from the stern of the ship.

Steve and Danny, fell to the deck, as three shots echoed in the silent night air. Jamal stood erect for a moment then dropped the AK and slumped to his knees. Blood ran from his mouth, as he turned to Jack, trying to speak. Another shot rang out, as Tom shot the kidnapper in the head.

Santosh and Gary, suddenly appeared over the side of the dhow. Danny turned to them and said, 'Oh nice, we're in the shit and you're off swimming.'

Tom, with Nicole now at his side, moved out onto the deck. She screamed Jack's name and ran to him.

'Zaikin!' she cried, when she saw him slumped against the pile of ropes.

She fell to her knees and pulled his head onto her lap. She bent down and kissed him gently, tears in her eyes. Her arm cradled his head, the other on his chest, she felt it move slowly up and down.

Tom was at his side and said, 'Take it easy, Jack,' then turning to the other guys shouted, 'Get something to stop the blood and get the chopper in. We need, Ian here *now*!'

With her face against his, she felt his warm, shallow, breath on her cheek. He opened his eyes and looked into hers, 'I love you, Nicole, I always will.'

'Shhh, Jack, don't talk, Zaikin,' as she held him close.

She felt the movement of his chest slow down and as the tears rolled down her cheeks and onto his face, her heart almost stopped as well. 'No! Please God. *No!*'

Epilogue

Dimitri Mikhailovich was on the huge veranda, looking out to sea, through the powerful tripod mounted telescope. His gaze fell on a sleek tri-masted yacht, sailing west towards the sunset. He moved the scope slightly and followed the beach round towards Nicole's villa. He adjusted the focus and saw his daughter seated on the lounger, her legs pulled up and her arms round them, in a semi foetal position. Dimitri moved the telescope slightly to the right and was suddenly surprised to see a man exit the villa and walk slowly towards his daughter.

* * *

Nicole did not hear the man approach. He stood behind her and placed his hands on her shoulders. She was frozen, she did not move. Then slowly his fingers moved around her neck and raised her face. She removed the big sunglasses and squinted slightly, as the rays of the setting sun caught her eyes. The man moved to her front, his hands still holding her face and neck. His face was in shadow, as he knelt by her side. Then slowly he moved closer to her and kissed her parted lips.

'Zaikin, why are you out of bed? Ten days ago you had a bullet in your liver. Ten days ago I thought you were dead. You're supposed to be resting.'

'I've rested long enough, darling. I want to make love to my wife.'

'I'm not your wife yet, Jack.'

'No, Nicole, but you soon will be.'

She dropped the sunglasses onto the sand, stood and gently slipped her arm around his waist, careful not to disturb the heavy bandages. He looked at her beautiful face, then kissed her, as they walked back to the villa.

* * *

On the veranda Dimitri let the telescope slip from his grasp, smiled and said, 'Moladitz, Jack. Well done, my boy.'

The End
(or is it?)

In the six months, following the rescue in the Gulf.....

Ali Wassam's wife and family were moved to Turkey. A one million dollar trust fund, has enabled her to buy a pleasant house close to her sister, in Istanbul. Her two daughters attend the best Muslim school in the city.

Santosh moved his family to the UK and lives in a country house in Berkshire. His three sons were enrolled in an exclusive private school and his mother and mother-in-law were brought over from India. He does not claim any social security benefits.

Ian Little and his partner, are still on the most expensive world cruise money can buy and are currently in Rio de Janeiro, enjoying themselves at the annual carnival.

Steve Shelby went to Thailand, and has bought shares in several holiday resorts, along Pattaya Beach. He decided against radical surgery to replace his lost eye and still wears the patch.

Danny Chaplain returned to Newcastle and moved his family into a large property on the 15th green, of his local golf club. He bought a six million pound Eurocopter, which his wife sent back. She has taken control of all the numbered accounts.

Tom Hillman and his wife Helen, are living in the Burgh Khalifa, while their new villa is being built, on the Palm, in Dubai. He spends most of his time out on the Gulf, in his new sixty foot yacht.

Lisa Reynard set up a pro bono academy for young aspiring journalists. She is living on Long Island, New York, close to her mother and is currently writing a novel, about a bunch of guys who find a couple of boxes of diamonds in the desert.

Dimitri Mikhailovich Orlov sold his first division London football club and bought a premier league club in Manchester. Olga continues to look after him.

Cancer Research UK, Save the Children Fund (India), The British Heart Foundation and UNICEF (Africa), each received, two hundred million dollars, from an anonymous benefactor.

Mr and Mrs Jack Castle have….
    Well, that's another story!

Printed in Great Britain
by Amazon

50246298R00163